W9-ADK-975

ENTER THREE WITCHES

CAROLINE B. COONEY

ENTER
THREE
WITCHES

A STORY OF MACBETH

SCHOLASTIC PRESS/NEW YORK

Text copyright © 2007 by Caroline B. Cooney All rights reserved. Published by Scholastic Press, an imprint of Scholastic Inc., *Publishers since 1920.* SCHOLASTIC, SCHOLASTIC PRESS, and associated logos are trademarks and/or registered trademarks of Scholastic Inc. No part of this publication may be reproduced, stored in a retrieval system, or transmitted in any form or by any means, electronic, mechanical, photocopying, recording, or otherwise, without written permission of the publisher. For information regarding permission, write to Scholastic Inc., Attention: Permissions Department, 557 Broadway, New York, NY 10012. Library of Congress Cataloging-in-Publication Data Cooney, Caroline B. Enter three witches : a story of Macbeth / by Caroline B. Cooney. – 1st ed. p. cm. ISBN-13: 978-0-439-71156-2 / ISBN-10: 0-439-71156-8 1. Macbeth, King of Scotland, 11th cent. – Fiction. 2. Regicides – Fiction. 3. Scotland – Fiction. I. Shakespeare, William, 1564–1616. Macbeth. II. Title. PS3553.O578E57 2007 813'54–dc22 2006015278 12 11 10 9 8 7 6 5 4 3 2 1 7 8 9 10 Printed in the U.S.A. First edition, April 2007 Book design by Kristina Albertson

ENTER

THREE

WITCHES

CHAPTER 1

Double, double, toil and trouble;
Fire burn, and cauldron bubble.
ACT IV, SCENE 1

IN THE COURTYARD, SOLDIERS GATHERED FOR WAR, BUT IN THE KITCHEN they were talking of witches. The kitchen staff did not care about kings and their wars.

Mary was torn. She didn't want to miss anything.

"I had to find the Weird Ones," Swin was saying. She didn't use the word *witch*. Most people wouldn't; it might summon one. "I went looking on the heath by myself last night."

Swin dared go on the moor at night? By herself? Mary would never do that. Out there, you were prey. Something stronger would get you. Elf-candles or dead-lights or ghosts.

Mary watched the young men strapping on their armor and thought of Asleif. At another castle her own father would be preparing to fight for the King, with Asleif at his side. Here the soldiers were running their thumbs down the newly sharpened blades of their swords. Some men were afraid. They might rather vanish into the Highlands, but they were trapped inside the high walls of Inverness Castle.

Swin wasn't afraid of anything. She was responsible for slaughtering meat for dinner and had spilled more blood than any warrior. They said Swin knew things that others didn't, so Mary had been thinking of asking Swin about the omen. Omens in the sky – like flying birds or falling stars – everyone understood those. But this omen was in Mary's hands.

The sleeves of Mary's sky-blue undergown were long and full, and she had pulled them down to cover her hands. They were pale, soft hands, because Mary did not have chores. The lines in her palms hardly showed, as if she hardly had a life. Her top gown was sleeveless and open to the waist, to show off the fine fabric of the dress beneath. Mary slid her arms in where her sash made a big front pocket and let her hands lie in the dark. Maybe her hands just needed rest, and when she took them out again, the omen would be gone.

The kitchen maids were breathless with excitement. They wouldn't dare go out on the moor and look for evil, either. "And were the Weird Ones there?" they asked Swin.

If Mary went into the kitchen, Swin would stop talking, because scullery maids didn't gossip in front of ladies. But then the trumpets started warming up. Mary did not want to miss what Swin was saying. She eased away from the courtyard, stepping backward down the stone hall toward the kitchens.

"*Three* sisters were there," said Swin casually.

Now Mary knew she meant witches — sisters was another safe way to name them.

"Three is a good number," explained Swin. "When a curse is needed, three winds up any charm you need."

Swin needed a curse? On whom? To do what?

Father Ninian preached against charms. He was upset because of that baby. Everybody was upset about the baby.

Swin teased the kitchen staff. "Guess what I have to bring the Weird Ones for them to lay a curse?"

Mary leaned forward to see what Swin, slaughterer of sheep, would take to witches.

Round about the cauldron go;
In the poisoned entrails throw.
ACT IV, SCENE 1

SWIN HAD SEEN THE EDGE OF THAT PALE BLUE GOWN ALL ALONG. How like a lady to think she was invisible when, in fact, she glowed. Swin didn't dislike Lady Mary — who meant nothing, just this year's ward of the castle — but Swin could not run the risk that Mary might tell on her. "Good morning, Lady

Mary," she called. "Saw you in the chapel at dawn," she added, because it was always good to let people know that you were watching. "Asking God for something?"

Lady Mary came into the kitchen. She was wearing a gown discarded by Lady Macbeth. In that same frosty winter blue, with her thick black braids hanging straight down to frame her white throat, Lady Macbeth had looked like some icy cold bird of prey. But Mary was Scottish in color, with auburn hair and hazel eyes. Her top gown was white and stiff, and she looked like a little girl playing nun. "I was praying for Asleif, Swin. That he and my father be in God's care."

They all crossed themselves.

Asleif was Lady Mary's betrothed. Mary loved to talk about him, so Swin knew that Mary had met him three times, and he was perfect, and marriage, when it came, would be perfect also. Asleif was squire to Lady Mary's father, the Thane of Cawdor. Squires were always getting killed in battle, since they held the lord's weapons and were apt to be in the way of the enemy's weapons. Swin wouldn't place a bet on Asleif's chances.

They were saying that the opposing armies were equal, which was bad; it meant longer fighting and more dying. But Swin tried to be kind. "Maybe Asleif will survive."

The wedding had been postponed, though Lady Mary was fourteen and old enough to be married. But here she was, still at Inverness, learning how to run a castle. Or, in this castle, not learning. At Inverness, there was but one mistress, and that lady did not share. Lady Macbeth loved every corner and stone of her world, and she kept complete control. She would never allow Lady Mary to do anything she herself liked doing nor anything a servant ought to do – which left nothing. Lady Mary just wandered aimlessly around the castle looking pretty and getting in the way.

The scullery maids were too interested in Swin's curse to remember that witches should not be talked of in front of Lady Mary. "Tell, Swin!" they demanded. "What did the Weird Ones ask for?"

A Weird One – the old word was *wyrd* – was a spell caster; a fate changer. Swin was not confident that fate could be changed. But sometimes a life had to be avenged, and for this Swin was willing to jeopardize her soul.

Swin liked an audience, and Lady Mary was as awestruck as the rest of them, her rosebud lips open with excitement. Swin wondered if Asleif would live to kiss those lips. She swept her listeners with hard eyes and slowly stirred an invisible pot, sniffed its invisible contents, and ladled invisible portions. The scullery maids and Lady Mary took their invisible cups, and didn't Lady Mary actually swallow her invisible brew? "The Weird Ones," said Swin, drawing out every syllable, "asked for things as always go in a witch's brew. First they want a rat without a tail."

Lady Mary shuddered.

But the kitchen girls were cross. "The stables are full of rats. We're always trying to kill rats. A rat without a tail is just a rat you didn't kill on the first stroke. What else do they require of you?" The girls frowned. Swin had better make it good.

. . . who, as others do,
Loves for his own ends, not for you.
ACT III, SCENE 5

ILDRED WAS DESPERATE. ONLY LADY MARY COULD HELP, AND THAT WAS the unfairest thing of all, because Ildred hated Lady Mary.

Ildred's parents had had nine children, and Ildred the last. By the time Ildred was fourteen and old enough for marriage, there was no money, no land, and no dowry. Ildred would have married anybody — even a fisherman by the sea or a shepherd in the hills. But her parents said that was beneath the family. They farmed her out to Lady Macbeth as a companion — Lady Macbeth, who needed no company but her husband. Ildred ran errands or did the hateful sewing for the beautiful gowns Lady Macbeth wore. And when the lady tired of these gowns, were they passed on to Ildred? No. They went to Lady Mary.

Lady Mary, an only child, who owned Shiel Castle in her own right and would one day own Cawdor Castle itself — and whose marriage to Asleif would bring Mary even *more* — *she* got the gowns. Mary was sober and careful and annoying. Most annoying of all, she was beautiful, glowing with eagerness for the world God had made. Men adored this.

When Mary entered the Great Hall, men looked at her for long, desiring moments and then pretended disinterest. Fostered to Lord and Lady Macbeth, Mary was therefore their legal ward.

The Macbeths would tear to pieces any man who behaved in an ungentlemanly way.

Men did not adore Ildred. She was nineteen now, and the one man she had thought loved her laughed at the mere idea and walked off. Only Ildred's dog loved her, and now she couldn't even keep Dirle safe.

Hundreds of soldiers – thrusting and jabbing their swords in the air, boasting of past and future prowess – any one of them might practice their aim on a wiggly little dog. Ildred had planned to tie up Dirle in the stable, but it was packed with kerns and stable hands, all disgusting and unreliable.

Lady Mary, of course, had a room of her own. Ildred didn't; Ildred was nothing, just a mender of hems.

Ildred was drowning in anger. She needed to confess this sin to Father Ninian, who would help her cast it away, but she could not admit, least of all to the sweet old priest, how desperate she felt, how many and huge were the things she wanted and would never have.

The only person who would understand was Lady Macbeth. Not the anger; Lady Macbeth always got her own way before she had to get angry. Their mistress was ruled by another emotion. Lady Macbeth was the wanting-est person Ildred had ever known – aching and yearning, scheming and dreaming . . . *wanting.*

It never crossed Lady Macbeth's mind that a meaningless half-servant like Ildred might want something, too.

Ildred walked slowly, conquering pain, and went to find Lady Mary.

S WIN'S SMILE WAS THIN AND BEAKY, LIKE A SWAN'S. HER EYES FLICK-
ered up and down the bodies of her listeners.

Swin would give *us* to those witches, thought Mary.

"They want a dog's tongue," said Swin. "Fresh."

Ildred flew into the kitchen. "Don't you dare touch my Dirle!"

"Keep your shoes on," said Swin. "I wouldn't take the tongue out
of some mangy old lapdog. I'd go after one of the hunting dogs."

If a hound of his got mutilated, Lord Macbeth would hang
Swin from the nearest tree. Unless the dogs – fierce enough to
kill a full-grown boar – killed her first. Mary said quickly, "You
mustn't go to those Weird Ones, anyway, Swin. It's wrong. If
you need help, say your prayers."

Swin spat in the fire to show what she thought of that prissy
little remark. "The witches help them that God won't."

Mary crossed herself, and the hand motion reminded her of
what she had come to ask Swin. It wasn't happening right now,
though. It came and went.

"I've shut Dirle in your room, Lady Mary," said Ildred, "so the
soldiers can't hurt him. But I can't lock the door. Give me the key."

Mary loved her tiny chamber, so brightly painted and lined
with such pretty draperies. Next to the rooms of Lord and Lady

Macbeth, it opened onto the high courtyard balcony and faced the morning sun. Or, since this was Scotland, the morning fog. She knew how badly Ildred wanted to share the room with her, and the trundle cot where harsh old Aelgitha had slept was unused.

Mary had come to Inverness with a servant her father had chosen, a woman who executed every task as if wishing to execute people instead. Suddenly last month, Aelgitha's son Fergus arrived. His little sons were ill, he said, and needed their grandmother to nurse them.

How could Mary say no to that? Aelgitha had so few possessions she didn't even pack. Mary gave them a purse to help pay for the doctor, and mother and son just walked away. The moment they were out of sight, the omen happened for the first time. Ever since then Mary had kept her thumbs tucked like packages inside her curled fingers.

Ildred was hard enough to tolerate by day. Mary did not want her company every night. "I don't have a key for the outside, Ildred. When I go to bed, I bolt it from the inside."

"There is a key," argued Ildred.

Mary nodded. "Lady Macbeth has it."

Only the lady of the castle had access to all the castle. Inverness required so many keys they clanked. Lady Macbeth kept them in a velvet waist pouch to silence them.

But today no one would dare interrupt Lady Macbeth about a dog. She was standing on the parapet, admiring the army her husband had gathered, because King Duncan had appointed her husband, great Lord Macbeth, to be commander.

In fact, the King had chosen two commanders, but Lady Macbeth just sniffed at the idea that her husband had an equal. Mary loved how Lady Macbeth loved Lord Macbeth. I will love Asleif just as much, she thought. And then, pitying Ildred, she said, "Dirle will be safe in my room. Swin, promise Ildred you will not touch Dirle."

Swin said nothing. She curled her lips in a twist, framed a silent word, and stirred her invisible stew.

Is she cursing someone? thought Mary.

They all looked down into the invisible pot, even Ildred, and the omen came back into Mary's hands.

There's daggers in men's smiles . . .
ACT II, SCENE 3

S EYTON HADN'T SLEPT. NOW AS THEY PREPARED TO MARCH, HIS heart raced. He'd practiced for this all his life, but so far he had never seen or been in a real battle.

Seyton was the fourth son, so there was neither land nor title left for him, but at least his father had arranged for him to be Lord Macbeth's squire. Who better to learn war from than the man who commanded it?

Up around the troops rose the high gray stone walls, grim even in the sun, grim even hung with flags and banners. Indoors, this was Lady Macbeth's castle, lovely and welcoming. But outside, it was a man's castle, built for war.

Someday – no matter what, no matter how – Seyton would have a place like this.

In the coming battle, Seyton must kill well and often, because King Duncan would give out rewards. It was hard to guess what these might be. The young men hoped for a little land or a minor title, but kings were unknowable. Seyton might get a mere silver tankard for all his troubles or an ivory-handled sword to hang on a wall.

Today they would face a local traitor, Macdonwald, and a foreign king, Norway. Norway was always trying to grab another piece of Scotland, and invasions required a local man, because somebody had to provide spies, anchorage, and food. Macdonwald had crossed over to Norway. Seyton yearned to be the one who killed Macdonwald, but that would never happen. He would be saved for one of the lords to kill.

Seyton was tired of hanging around.

They couldn't march until the tottering old priest gave the blessing. Seyton had no use for priests. He wanted action.

. . . his Majesty went into the field . . .
ACT V, SCENE 1

MARY'S FIRST BETROTHAL HAD BEEN TO AN ISLAND BOY WHO routinely climbed the sea cliffs to get the tastiest birds' eggs from their nests. Davey had been a fine cragsman, so brave and daring – until he fell. Davey would hate

Mary to say that he fell. He did not fall: The stones to which he clung ripped away from the cliff, and he went down with them. He had been eleven years old. They weren't able to retrieve his body because of the vicious rocks and the wicked sea, and she thought of his little bones sometimes, thrashing in the tide.

The voice of Macbeth blasted like a trumpet down the stone hall that separated the kitchen from the rest of the castle. "Down with the traitor Macdonwald!"

"Down with the traitor!" his men shouted back.

Mary's heart hurt.

Macdonwald was a fine man – the father, in fact, of Mary's dead Davey. Davey had been his only son, and the loss of Davey had been the loss of everything. Macdonwald became a different man. If Lord Macbeth and King Duncan had their way, he would become a dead man.

Mary could not help grieving for Macdonwald's dear wife and daughters. What would become of them? Nothing good. "Dear Lord," she prayed, facing the cross on the wall, "protect them. Macdonwald has done a terrible thing, but have pity."

And then, although men never bothered with kitchens and certainly not when headed off to war, Lord Macbeth's squire, Seyton, strode into the room, weapons and armor clanking. He rarely glanced at Mary, but Mary often glanced at him. He was lean and broad-shouldered, with a teasing smile and laughing eyes. His hair was very fashionable, trimmed short in front, but with long curled locks behind. When Mary couldn't precisely remember what Asleif looked like, she liked to think he looked like Seyton.

It happened again. Her thumbs were pricking. It was like being bitten by the tiny sharp teeth of bats. Mary stared at her thumbs and willed it to stop. Sometimes when she sat too long in one position, perhaps embroidering in the solar, her foot would fall asleep, and when the foot woke up, it tingled unpleasantly. But her thumbs? It couldn't be a good omen. Her sins were small – refusing to share a room – but perhaps not small to God. Was God angry?

Seyton surveyed the scullery maids. "All these lovely girls, all in one place," said Seyton, who flirted with anything in a long gown. "Even the beautiful little Lady Mary," he added, bowing.

Mary's thumbs actually hurt. She wanted to put them in her mouth and suck on them, as if she had snakebite. She couldn't think of anything to say to Seyton, which was always the case, because she felt such anxiety around him. At one and the same time, she wanted to sit in his lap and slam the door in his face.

Swin folded her muscular arms over her large chest. "Not ready for war, are you, Seyton?" she said. "Look at you. Cheeks white as linen. Scared, I suppose. Doesn't surprise me, a cream-faced loon like you."

A scullery maid dared speak like that to the son of a noble? Mary should report Swin to Lady Macbeth. But Ildred would do it. Ildred loved reporting people.

Seyton, however, was laughing. Perhaps he and Swin were just flirting. Mary did not understand flirting.

A kern stuck his head into the kitchen. Mary was afraid of kerns, who were little more than slaves drafted into the army. They went first and died the most. "The priest," he warned them. "About to give his benison."

"Mustn't miss the blessing," said Seyton. "All of us need it. Except you, of course, Lady Mary. You are already blessed." He offered Mary his arm, but Swin flipped her huge knife so the sharp side was toward Seyton and brought the blade slowly up between Seyton's extended arm and Lady Mary.

She'd chop his hand off, thought Mary, shocked.

Could it be against *Seyton* that Swin wanted her curse?

The trumpets exploded in a brassy shout to the world that Macbeth was coming to save King Duncan. Mary loved to think of kings, and certainly wanted Duncan's army to have God's benison, so she slid her red slippers into wooden pattens and clogged across the muddy courtyard without wetting her feet. Behind her came Swin, who was barefoot inside her wooden shoes, and then the scullery maids, who had no shoes.

The sky was that blue found only in heaven or on the ceilings of churches. Against this, the stone-piled castle had a dark, fierce beauty. Macbeth stood alone on the battlements, hair blowing in the wind. "Death to Norway!" he roared.

Norway had always owned the far north of Scotland and the far-flung islands of Shetland and Orkney, but naturally Norway wanted more. Everybody wanted more. Especially Lady Macbeth. There was nothing the lady did not want, and no peace for her husband until he obtained it. Even then, she only wanted more.

Lady Macbeth stood just enough to the side that she did not trespass on her husband's glory but increased it. The wind whipped her scarlet gown with its bands of yellow, as if she herself were a flag for him. Her hands were clasped over her heart — not in prayer but in pride. Mary ran up to join the lady, but the balcony was too crowded. She found herself squashed in a corner where she could hardly see a thing and certainly couldn't hear Father Ninian, whose whispery old voice even God must struggle to hear.

Mary prayed hard for King Duncan, whom she had never seen. They said he was great of heart, which all kings should be but never were.

<hr />

. . . some danger does approach you nearly.
ACT IV, SCENE 2

<hr />

SWIN HAD BEEN STEALING FOOD FOR A YEAR NOW.

A servant who robbed her master would hang. Swin knew this and robbed anyway. Not one servant, stable hand, soldier, or silly little foster daughter worried Swin. Lady Macbeth was the difficulty. Lady Macbeth was as beautiful as a hawk in flight, and like the hawk she saw the smallest activity and pounced. When she couldn't see with her own sharp eyes, she used informers. Ildred was one.

Swin was pleased with herself, setting up that story of witches. They were out there, and Swin yearned to set a curse through them, but she had no time for it now. However, if she got caught carrying meat from the castle, she'd say those witches had demanded it for their stew. Everybody but Lady Macbeth might even believe her.

When all eyes were on the departing army, Swin retreated to her kitchen and walked out the back door. She passed the scullery and the little yard where she kept hens and geese penned up. The geese chatted eagerly, because they liked Swin, not knowing she planned to serve them for dinner. Swin left the castle by the work gate. Lord Macbeth must feel very sure that the battle would stay on the seashore where it belonged, because he had not dropped the portcullis nor even posted a guard.

She drifted between sheets drying on lines, sauntered past old outbuildings and barns, and came out on a narrow path, which led to the moor.

Her only family was her grandfather, crippled from a hunting accident. He would not leave the tiny low hut where he had spent his life. Until last year, he could still fish, catch game in snares, and tend a few sheep. But his eyes had whitened, as old men's do, and he was blind. Without Swin, he had no hope. Once caught, she had no hope, either.

She massaged her neck, the one that would break when they hanged her for this. She walked casually over a hill, down a vale, and into the crooked trees. Then she ran. She must be back before she was missed, and she had miles to go.

. . . come, Fate, into the list . . .

ACT III, SCENE 1

A GREAT VOICE IS THE MARK OF A GREAT MAN. WHEN MACBETH'S shout filled the ears of a thousand men, Mary loved him, and so did the troops, who cheered and stomped. The fight would be northeast of Inverness, where Norway's fleet had anchored. From her position on the battlement, Mary couldn't see that direction. She was facing the valley of the River Ness, where it flowed brown and muddy from its loch. In the distance, blue hills piled on top of one another. Mary was swept by love for her beautiful Scotland. She lifted her face once more to God and prayed for those she loved. And then, because she felt safer with saints, she prayed to Saint Hilda and Saint Margaret. They were halfway to God and more likely to hold her hand. She asked them to care for her father and for Asleif, and even for the family of Macdonwald. "Amen," she finished. When she opened her eyes, she saw Swin far below, striding toward the heath. A large leather sack was hanging from her shoulder.

Mary knew what was in that sack, and who wanted it.

What if Swin found those witches? And got her curse? What if it was on Seyton? A witch could grab Seyton's own lance so it went backward into his heart, or force Seyton's horse to throw him and break his back, or change the tide so it drowned him.

What if, at the moment Lord Macbeth needed Seyton, the curse came true?

The curse of Swin could lose this battle.

And then Lady Mary of Shiel had a horrible thought. Since before dawn, she herself had been praying for the King's own enemy – Macdonwald the traitor. It could be her prayer that turned the battle against her dear Lord Macbeth.

While Mary dithered, Swin vanished.

The moor was like that. It consumed people. The bogs were pretty, green, and dangerous. And the cliffs and rocks, the endless heather – they smirked as you lost yourself. Hiding among them were lepers or poor people not worth saving or robbers escaping their hangings. And of course, the lost souls, the unburied. Their clutching fingers were the strongest, their voices the most dangerous to hear.

I have to stop Swin, thought Mary, and she went down two flights of stone stairs and out through the kitchen, past the geese, and onto the moor.

The path narrowed and swerved. Every bush had thorns, and every tree bent low. Fields grew stone instead of grass. In tiny brooks, water smacked on rocks like a hand against a cheek. How fast could Swin be going? Why hadn't Mary caught up?

She passed small cottages with walls of turf and roofs thatched in heather. Of course there were no windows. Out here, spirits were always circling, especially in thunder and lightning. They could not be given entrance to a house where children slept.

Am I still a child? thought Mary. Surely not. Surely I am old enough to wed now. After the victory, Father will send for me and Asleif will take me home.

Asleif's castle was called Gledstane. These days they pronounced it "glad stone." Mary loved to picture her life there, built on stone and always glad.

An old hag came out a tiny door. The peat smoke of her fire wrapped around her like a cloak. "Don't go on, lass," said the woman. "Path ends here. Us is the last cottage."

"I'm looking for someone," explained Mary.

"Isn't *someone* you'll find on that heath. Is *something*."

The heather shivered, as if invisible feet were running through it. "There they are," said the hag, pointing.

But Mary saw where Swin's long skirt had dragged over that damp grass and made a dry path. Easy to follow, almost an invitation.

Mary forgot the old woman and ran on into heather as dark as spilled wine. Here and there glittered the crystal waterfall of a mountain burn. And then the trail was gone. Gone the blue sky and the singing bird. Even the heather was gone. Mist rearranged her hair and played with her gown. It felt like fingers.

"Swin!" she called.

Swin, breathed the fog.

Mary turned in a slow circle. Everywhere, the moor was the same. Nowhere was there a path. She was lost where stones were known to move and trees to speak. *Saint Hilda before me,* she prayed. *Saint Margaret behind me.*

You had to be careful with prayers like that. You might leave something out, and evil would reach its damp and curling hand through the hole.

Maybe she would find a hut where a friendly peasant would take her in . . . except that anyone who lived here had no friends and would not be a friend.

Out of the fog appeared a tiny church. Who would build a church here, dark and at the bottom of things?

The church was broken up and broken into. Could anything be more terrible than an abandoned church? A place where God once lived, and now rats made a home?

Saint Hilda and Saint Margaret, be with me, prayed Mary.

Out of the ruins came three creatures. They were not Saint Hilda or Saint Margaret.

CHAPTER 2

Be lion-mettled, proud . . .
ACT IV, SCENE 1

F LEANCE HAD TUGGED ON HIS BEST HOSE, IN THE COLORS HIS CLAN always wore: dark green with wide yellow bands. Over these went soft yellow deerskin boots that he tied beneath his knees, flexing his legs to be sure he could maneuver. Carefully he tucked his dirk under his belt, so the blade would show how dangerous he was. Fleance, only son of Banquo, captain of King Duncan's army, had been swaggering for days. He would fight by his father's side. Together, they would vanquish the foe.

Lord Macbeth appeared over the hill with *his* troops. Fleance hated to admit that King Duncan had appointed two commanders in this war, but it was so. And then his father said, as if it didn't matter, as if Fleance should have known, "You're too young, Fleance. You can watch, but you can't fight."

Not fight? Fleance was scrawny, but this was *war* – the King needed him! He had to be in this!

"Brude!" yelled Banquo. A squire rode over eagerly, expecting some fine assignment. "Take care of my little boy."

Fleance burned with shame. He was fourteen. Other boys too young for beards would be fighting.

Banquo pointed to a broad, flowery meadow that sloped up from the sand. "Keep him safe and out of danger," Banquo ordered, and he rode away to join Macbeth.

Out of danger? Danger was the point! Fleance was crushed. He yearned to disobey his father, but he never had; he didn't even know anyone who had disobeyed a father. Fleance always liked Scriptures in church where sons rebelled, a favorite activity among Biblical sons. Even King David couldn't make his sons obey. But this was Scotland, not Jerusalem, and in the Highlands, a son did what he was told.

His father's poor squire looked beseechingly at the sky, as if hoping God would intervene, but God didn't. Brude muttered something under his breath that sounded like "worm" – meaning Fleance – meaning, *Everybody else gets to fight, and I have to stay with this fish bait?*

They were both mounted. Fleance had the finer horse, but Brude sat taller and more easily. Most men sat taller and more easily than Fleance. Ahead of them, kerns were being herded down onto the hard sand. They had battle-axes and lances but not armor. Kerns weren't worth it. They would do their part and then die, and that's what they were for. And yet *they* got to be in the battle, and Fleance didn't.

His father, who was to control the right wing, rode out of sight.

There was but one other man who stayed safe and could only watch – King Duncan himself. The King's person could not be at risk. Fleance agreed with that because a king was sacred, but the two princes got to fight. Why weren't they sacred? Probably because Duncan had not actually named either one as his heir. Right now Malcolm and Donalbain were just sons, the way other people were just sons, like Fleance, for example – who ought to be at his father's side! And the princes weren't much older than Fleance! Well, Malcolm was probably twenty-five, but Donalbain was seventeen. *He* got to fight! Fourteen wasn't that much younger.

Lord Macbeth was wheeling his horse among the men, shouting orders. When Macbeth had sons, he'd probably let them fight when they were *ten*.

Fleance's horse was bored and began to graze.

Norwaymen poured off their ships onto a wide stretch of hard sand. Reluctantly, moving only because officers on horseback prodded them with swords, the kerns approached the enemy.

"We could get closer," said Fleance.

"No," said Brude, who was so eager to get closer he was twitching from jaw to thigh. He had spent his life preparing for such a battle and now was forced to be nurse to a spoiled, useless son.

The troops of Norway were out of the water, expecting a decent amount of time to draw up and arrange themselves. But Macbeth came down like an eagle on lambs, screaming the war cry of the Highlands. The power of his charge thrilled even the kerns, and they raced forward with him. The armies met hideously, face-to-face, no room to move, no hope except to kill. His thundering voice filling the beachfront, Macbeth fought from his horse, carving a passage through enemy flesh. Blood was flung like rain.

"His sword smokes!" yelled Brude.

Macbeth was not simply fighting – he had some destination in mind and didn't care how many Norwaymen got in his way. Fleance squinted for longer sight. Far beyond Macbeth, he recognized the banner of the man Macbeth intended to reach: Macdonwald. With whom every Scots noble here had supped and raised sons. A traitor.

Fleance could not imagine a man turning traitor. Loyalty was part of every oath and every day. To be loyal was the greatest virtue. How did the thought of betraying your king even enter your mind?

When Duncan was acclaimed King, the people built altars of stone for Saint Hilda and Saint Margaret, each with its relic: the hand of one and the heart of the other. By these saints, every lord said his oath to Duncan. An oath sworn on two saints could not be broken, but Macdonwald was breaking it. He'd have no saint by his side in this battle.

The two captains met on the sand: traitor Macdonwald and loyal Macbeth. The kerns of each faction backed away to give them space and watch the fight. Two armies boiled down to two men. If the kerns were lucky, the battle would be decided by this duel, and they would get home alive.

Fleance expected a long fight, full of thrusts and jabs, wounds and near misses, but it was not to be. Macbeth simply lifted his claymore, the huge double-sided sword Fleance could not yet handle, and brought it down, splitting Macdonwald from jaw to belly.

Few men had that strength or resolve. His father, Banquo, would have taken Macdonwald prisoner, but Lord Macbeth had no interest in prisoners.

"It's over," whispered Brude, impressed but sorry.

Brude was wrong. The death of Macdonwald enraged the Norwaymen. They fought twice as hard and seemed suddenly to have twice the men. From the high slant of the meadow, Brude and Fleance could see Norway's plan: Surround Macbeth and execute him as he had executed Macdonwald.

Fleance shouted a warning, but no one could hear over the din of battle.

"I could help!" said Brude desperately. "If only I –"

"I release you," said Fleance. "Fight."

Brude howled a scream-song and plunged into the Norwaymen, who whirled, crouching, to meet this attack from the rear.

When they saw but one man, they laughed, and cut Brude down easily and swiftly. But his death had purpose: Macbeth's men were given time to shift position. Now it was the Norwaymen who were cut off.

Fleance took up the battle howl, perhaps in horror at Brude's quick end or pride in Scotland's quick reaction, or maybe just to add himself to the battle in some way. It was a mistake. Two of the enemy looked up and recognized the yellow and green of Banquo. "Death to Lochaber!" they screamed, using a title of his father's. Running like deer, they leaped up the slight overhang between meadow and sand, where grass hung like long hair, to kill the son of Banquo.

Fleance had sharpened his sword. It was ready. But he, having accepted his father's order, was unready. He could not seem to get the sword out of its scabbard, and his horse, frightened by the two figures lunging toward it, skittered sideways. He grabbed its mane so he wouldn't be thrown off. Fleance was not a fine rider.

The first enemy lifted his ax to slice the horse's throat. Killing the horse was the first step in killing the rider, who would now be down and helpless, but since the horse was dancing around, the enemy's ax chopped grass.

Finally, Fleance got his sword out. He swung wildly and missed so badly he frightened his own horse, which reared violently. Keeping his seat now took both hands. Fleance dropped his weapon.

The two attackers laughed, swung their axes again, and sliced through the legs of his horse. It buckled, hitting the ground, rolling in agony, and pinning Fleance by the leg. At least he had fallen on his back so the death stroke would enter his chest. A Scottish father would not even bury a son who died a coward.

The enemy waved dirks in his face, giving him a few seconds to fear what was coming.

But what came was a Scottish warrior swinging a Scottish ax.

Seyton, Macbeth's squire! Seyton decapitated the one and stabbed the second in the back. This one, dead but still gripping his dirk, fell on top of Fleance. I'm saved, but I'll die anyway, thought Fleance.

But the blade missed his heart and lungs and ripped through his shoulder.

Fleance was joyful. He would have a battle scar.

Thrice the brindled cat hath mewed.
ACT IV, SCENE 1

HREE OF THEM. ROCKING AND MOCKING. FACING MARY, IF THOSE could be called faces. Weird Ones who were weird beyond any imagining.

What had they done with Swin? There was no sign of her. Behind the Weird Ones burned a fire, but no cauldron hung over it. It had begun to rain. The rain did not put out the fire or even dampen it.

One of them cradled a calico cat, which also stared at Mary, tail switching, eyes glowing. The witch's face was covered with warts, and from each wart sprouted a hair. A witch should be able to get rid of her own warts. But perhaps witches were proud of their warts.

Father Ninian said the devil didn't need to commit evil himself. The devil suggested evil, and you, being weak, did it on your own. I must not be weak, Mary told herself. But she was weak, from her eyes, which had filled with tears, to her knees, which were quivering. "I came for Swin," whispered Mary. Swin had planned to bring them presents. Rats without tails and such. "I have nothing to give," said Mary nervously.

"Nothing is required." This one was withered like a tree. Her skin looked like bark. Her necklace was made of teeth. Human teeth.

The second one raised her head, and her tangled hair rearranged itself, like vines in a wind. Her ears sharpened, as if she were a hound scenting a fox. "We are called," she told her sisters.

The three turned to face a sound Mary could not hear. "Is it Swin?" she said. "May Swin come home with me?"

"Thrummmmm," whispered the first Weird One.

"Drummmmm," whispered the next.

The third bared her rotted teeth at Mary. "Runnnnn!"

. . . I have bought
Golden opinions from all sorts of people . . .
ACT I, SCENE 7

LORD BANQUO TORE HIS OWN TUNIC TO BANDAGE HIS SON'S WOUND. It wasn't deep, but it was bleeding heavily. He cleaned the wound vigorously, which hurt, and then tied the bandage so tight it hurt even more. Fleance tried not to show the pain.

"Fleance was brilliant," said Seyton carelessly. "He killed that one on the sand. I just finished this other one off for him."

Fleance was thrilled and dismayed by these lies and could not look at his father. He knew the false picture was a great gift to Banquo: his son, the warrior.

Lord Banquo looked down at the dead man with the knife in his back. A man's clan or country could be known by clothing, but hair was also a marker. Scotsmen liked their hair short over the forehead and long over the neck. Norwaymen neither cut nor combed their hair, but left it wild and untended. As the years went by, the hair itself became fearsome. The man at their feet had neatly trimmed shoulder-length hair in back. Seyton turned the body over with his foot. The man's fine cloak spilled around him, straining at the clasp of a gold pin as big as the palm of a hand. Norwaymen did not work in gold.

"Traitor," said Seyton, spitting on the dead man's face.

"He *was* a traitor," said Lord Banquo. "Now he belongs to God." Banquo sighed, staring down the long shelf of sand, counting the cost of battle. It was high. "Duncan is a good man and a good king," said Fleance's father sadly. "I remain amazed that anyone rebelled against him. But Macdonwald has ached for power all his life. Perhaps without a son to steady him, power was all that mattered."

Fleance loved to ponder things and wanted to think about power, but Seyton said proudly, "Lord Macbeth split Macdonwald in half."

"I saw," said Banquo. "Norway has agreed to pay ten thousand to King Duncan for the privilege of burying these men. May there be no more battles between us."

Fleance didn't want his father sounding weak in front of Seyton. Seyton was everything Fleance yearned to be: strong, fearless, and quick, good with horses, and easy with girls. And now he had saved Fleance's life, and Fleance owed him. "King Duncan will honor you, Seyton, for your excellent fighting," he said quickly. Now was the time to admit that Seyton had been the warrior. He took a breath and girded himself for the truth.

But Fleance was trapped by his father's intense pride. "You, my son, must also have honor," said Banquo, leaning over the corpse. He removed the gold pin and put it on Fleance as trophy and sign of the kill. Then he, who was rarely demonstrative, kissed his son's forehead. Fleance felt the kiss like a burn. He hadn't earned it.

And yet – now he could stand before his king as a man. A warrior who had fought for him, had been loyal and true – and had lied. Fleance started to remove the brooch and tell the truth, but his father mounted his horse, calling over his shoulder, "I go with Macbeth to report to the King. You and Seyton assist with the removal of our dead."

Not see King Duncan's joy when the captains made their report? Not stand next to Prince Malcolm and Prince Donalbain and bask in their admiration? Fleance kicked the sand like a little boy made to go to bed early – and the person who saw him was Macbeth.

Macbeth looked Fleance up and down, shrugged as if Fleance were so much seaweed, and caught up with Banquo.

I don't even have a horse, thought Fleance. I'll have to walk. Like some kern.

His shoulder really hurt now. He took one step. The leg that had been caught under the horse didn't feel so good, either.

"Don't worry about the burials," Seyton told Fleance, taking rings off a dead hand. "The men will do it."

Kerns were already burying kerns up in the meadow where, a few hours ago, Fleance's horse had grazed. Nobody cared about the kerns, who were just livestock. Nobody even bothered to find out their names. The body of Brude was flung in among them.

If we had followed my father's orders, Brude would be alive, thought Fleance. But if Brude hadn't charged, maybe Macbeth would be dead.

"The best thing is to kill your own man, Fleance," said Seyton. "You won your spurs there."

Fleance flushed. He had won nothing.

"We won't talk about it again," said Seyton. His tone was not comforting. It hung heavily, like a cloud over the sea. Fleance looked into Seyton's eyes and saw that Seyton owned a piece of him now — a sad, cowardly piece — a piece that took the credit for deeds others had done.

But when Seyton grinned, Fleance lost track of his confusion. It was a wonderful grin, full of friendship and laughter.

"There's another fine thing soon to come," said Seyton. "Girls love a warrior. Doesn't matter if they're a lady or a laundress. You tell them you killed your man, and they'll give you anything you want."

What Fleance wanted was not to have lied to his father about anything as valuable as honor.

. . . why do you start and seem to fear
Things that do sound so fair?
ACT I, SCENE 3

MARY OBEYED THE WITCH'S ORDER. SHE RAN. SHE DIDN'T GET far. Her feet tangled in her skirt, and she tripped and hit the ground hard. Heather looked soft and cushiony, but it grew on rocks. Beneath her bruised body, the ground throbbed. Were the witches pounding after her? Was *she* the ingredient they lacked?

Mary looked back even though it might turn her to salt. Coming out of the mist, darkly silhouetted against that orange fire, were two soldiers on horseback.

Soldiers were worse than witches. Men excited from fighting could not wind down. And these were no ordinary Scottish ponies – they were massive chargers. Mary flattened herself.

Thin as a bird lost in the wind came a long, shivery cry: "Hail, Macbeth!" A weird sound from weird mouths.

Macbeth? How extraordinary. Where was his squire, Seyton? Where were Lord Ross and Lord Lennox and the other officers? Could Macbeth have lost them in the mist? Had Mary been on the moor so long that the battle had been waged? Had it been lost or won?

Her thumbs pricked.

"*Hail, Thane of Glamis,*" the Weird Ones wailed.

Glamis was the castle Macbeth inherited when his father died. Twice Mary had had the privilege of staying there. Lords moved with the seasons, from one stronghold to another, collecting rents, conducting law courts, hunting deer, and giving feasts. When the food at one castle was eaten up and the privies were over-flowing, a lord traveled on to the next. Presently, the Macbeths were at Inverness, which Mary liked almost as much as her own castle at Shiel.

Now the witches were calling a different tune. *"All hail the Thane of Cawdor."*

The man with Macbeth was her very own father? Mary sat up. She peered through the mist. It was like seeing through rags. The soldiers were staring at the witches, and the witches were staring at the soldiers. Nobody looked Mary's way.

It was not her father. The man with Macbeth was Lord Banquo. Even more strange. *Both* commanders? Where were their armies?

"Thane of Cawdor," the Weird Ones repeated, pointing at Macbeth.

They aren't very good seers, thought Mary, if they can't even tell who's standing in front of them.

"I am Thane of Glamis," Macbeth agreed cheerfully, "but not Cawdor." He seemed entertained, as one watching a skit at the fair. "The Thane of Cawdor lives – a gentleman of prosperity and in good health."

Mary smiled.

"No," said the first witch. "He is none of that. Hail to thee, Thane of Cawdor."

Ribbons of fog stood up and waved, like a crowd of people half there.

"All hail Macbeth," cried the witches, "who shall be king here-after."

The word *king* hung in the air. Even the flames of the fire seemed to spell king and the hot breath of the horses to echo it. *King*. Mary could have reached up and taken the word in her hand.

King.

"My turn, you skinny old hags," said Banquo, who was chuck-ling. "Look into the seeds of time," he teased, "and tell *my* fate."

"You, Banquo? You will be lesser than Macbeth, and greater. Not so happy, yet happier. Sire of kings, but not king yourself."

The ruins of the church wavered in the fog. The pointed arches slipped from sight, and the Weird Ones shivered, coming and going in the damp. And then they went.

"Stay!" called Macbeth. "Tell us more! Why did you stop us on this blasted heath of yours?"

Blasted was a double word: It meant windblown but also cursed. Mary was afraid of the word. She lay back so the captains couldn't see her. Her spine pressed against the hard little knots of twisted heather. She felt evil coming up from under the stony ground – where hell lay.

Macbeth turned his horse in a full circle, but he didn't see the witches and he didn't see Mary.

"We imagined it," suggested Banquo. "Unless, of course, they're right and they do know everything, and you, my friend, are going to be king. Not to mention Thane of Cawdor. Isn't that how the song went?"

But Mary heard another song. It was the witches singing under the earth:

When shall we three meet again, in thunder, lightning, or in rain?
When the hurly-burly's done, when the battle's lost and won.

Mary tried to get up and couldn't. She was rooted to the spot.

"Lord Macbeth! Banquo!" came normal shouts from normal throats. "It's Ross! Where are you? The King sent us to find you! Here we win the finest victory anyone could ask for, and you two ride off on some errand?"

The little valley filled with soldiers and horses and the wild, proud laughter of men who had won. "Tonight we rest at Forres, the King's palace," said Lord Ross excitedly, "but tomorrow we go to Inverness. King Duncan will pay both of you the honors you earned today. But the first honor, my lord Macbeth, is mine. I am privileged to report that *you* are now the Thane of Cawdor."

Beneath Mary, the earth softened. The Weird Ones began to pull her down.

Puzzled, Macbeth said, "The Thane of Cawdor lives."

"For the moment. It turns out there were *two* traitors. Not just Macdonwald. Cawdor also went over to Norway. We captured him. King Duncan has given the order. Cawdor will be executed tomorrow."

The instruments of darkness tell us truths . . .

ACT I, SCENE 3

WHEN SWIN GOT BACK TO THE CASTLE, LADY MACBETH still stood on the parapet, watching the horizon. It seemed to Swin that she had run all the way to her grandfather's and back, had been away no time at all, and yet the sun had crossed the sky. Swin had the sense of time snatched from her hands and given to others.

The forecourt was busy. There was no village at Inverness, so the castle was everything to the people in that countryside – a marketplace, for mutton or marriage; a court; a chapel. On holy days, the feasts were held here. But today there was just the waiting. Who would win? Who would die?

Lady Macbeth spoke over their heads. "There will be a victory feast," she said, as if she knew, had read it in the sky. "Not tonight. I doubt they can return from battle that quickly. Tomorrow night or the following."

The lady could be a witch herself, thought Swin, knowing so much beforehand.

"We at Inverness will host the feast," said Lady Macbeth.

Since half the staff had gone with Lord Macbeth, the rest would have double the work to feed so many soldiers.

"Our gracious king will join us," said Lady Macbeth.

No king had ever slept at Inverness. No one here had even *seen* this king for whom men were laying down their lives. Even Swin was excited.

"And his sons, our dear princes, will be here also."

Swin thought of princes and how they sometimes fell in love with ordinary girls.

"My husband commanded this battle, and every man of mark will be here to honor him."

Swin was amused. Co-commander Banquo was meaningless to Lady Macbeth. Even the King was meaningless to Lady Macbeth. Her husband was finer than both of them and deserved more.

"Jennet, shovel the old rushes out of the hall. Edwin, scrub the stones. Fhiora, fresh rushes, scented with marjoram. Ian, clean up this courtyard. No horse droppings. Swin, a feast fit for a king. Ildred, see to the tablecloths. Polish the goblets."

Even in great houses, only the lord and lady had their own goblets. On the benches below, they would be five or six to a tankard. Last year Lady Macbeth decided every guest at her table must have his own, and immediately Lord Macbeth gave his wife what she wanted. It didn't keep Lady Macbeth from wanting more; she was always in a state of wanting.

Ildred, who never knew when to be silent, spoke up. "Since that woman Aelgitha does not seem to be returning, my lady, and since there is space in Lady Mary's chamber —"

"No," said Lady Macbeth curtly. She was always curt with Ildred, who annoyed her, and Ildred therefore was always curt with the servants.

Swin was not a person who felt pity. If she were to pity the pigs and lambs she slaughtered, there would be precious little dinner on the table. But Swin pitied Ildred.

"We will have many guests," said Lady Macbeth. "The King, of course, will sleep in our chamber, which is worthy of him. Lady Mary's room will suit the princes."

Which left both Lady Mary and Ildred without a place to sleep, a problem of no interest to Lady Macbeth, any more than the possibility of wounded men interested her. She was entertaining a king, not worrying about bandages. Swin would tear up the shabby old tablecloths in the cupboard. She went into the kitchen to check the supply of vinegar, for washing wounds, and thought about that servant Aelgitha's departure.

Her son claimed his babies needed nursing. But when Swin had offered a physic, good for sick babes, Aelgitha shook her head. "No one is sick. It's just time to leave." And she left.

Time to leave? Swin had thought. We are servants. We do not decide when to stay and when to leave. Swin didn't tell on Aelgitha, because she never told on anybody; she was committing too many crimes herself. But she pondered it.

In the great outdoor fireplace, Swin began the long, slow roasting of an ox. The rich, meaty scent made the penned-up hounds howl and moan. Ildred went past, Dirle at her side, to take the clean linens from the line. Swin cut off a chunk of meat for the dog. No hope she'd ever be friends with Ildred, but a dog was friend to all who fed him.

Swineherds brought their fattest pigs. The steward went down to the river to buy trout and salmon. Bakers prepared heavy brown bread whose slices would be plates for the soldiers, and sweet white bread for the officers. Goat cheese and sheep's milk were toted from the stone room over the cold spring and kegs of ale were rolled out.

And a letter came for Lady Macbeth. Swin had never seen a letter. She dropped everything, rushing to look, but Lady Macbeth kept it cradled in her hands and close to her heart. Slowly, the lady climbed the inner stair to the wide balcony that ran from castle wall to castle wall. Then she held the letter to her lips and kissed it, as Father Ninian kissed the Gospel.

How goes the world, sir, now?
ACT II, SCENE 4

THE RAIN STOPPED.
The men left.
Even the Weird Ones scorned Mary's company and released her from the soil.

Mary was alone in all the ways there were to be alone on a blasted heath. She, too, was blasted: She was now the daughter of a traitor.

They heard me on the parapet praying for my father's success, thought Mary. They will think I knew. They will say I could have told Macbeth and didn't.

They will say I am likewise a traitor who must die.

CHAPTER 3

Fair is foul, and foul is fair.
ACT I, SCENE 1

I F MARY WENT BACK TO INVERNESS, SHE WOULD BE SCORNED FIRST AND hanged second. Mary had seen hangings. No matter how brave you were, your body wasn't. It kicked and thrashed and fought. Often the crowd laughed to watch it. Or maybe they'd cut off Mary's head. She'd have to rest her cheek on the old stump where Swin normally brought an ax down on the neck of some struggling hen.

Better to go home to Cawdor, sunny and bright, where friends and cousins and dogs filled the castle and the walls were thick. Mary ran fast and hard, as if she could outdistance fate. "Asleif," she cried. "Come and get me!" But sure as Davey's bones still thrashed in the sea, Asleif had fought beside her father and died there.

Mary peered through the mist, as if she actually knew what direction Cawdor was and had some hope of getting there. Mother died so long ago, she thought. All these years, a castle without a woman. It's probably grim and filthy. And empty. Our men would have gone to war with Father. That's what your tenants are – your soldiers. They, too, must be dead on the beach. Every man I knew and loved: the stewards, the shepherds, the farm boys.

She was almost glad when she remembered that Cawdor was no longer hers. She would go to Shiel instead, the estate she had inherited from her mother's family. Shiel lay on the soft side of Scotland, where the saints built chapels, the grass grew green, and flocks of sheep burbled like foam in a stream. When fires were lit at Shiel, the people smiled and told long stories.

She would walk through the night. This far north, summer nights never grew fully dark. She could see the road before her . . . although she would be alone in the half-night: the gloaming, in whose dim shadows kelpies and ghosts and dead-lights waited. Their fingers would stroke her bare skin, and the ribbons of their breath would twine around her neck and –

The mist lifted. Sun shone gold on flowers and silver on streams. Mary smelled wild thyme and peat smoke, heard sheep baa-ing and birds twittering. The world was alive and bright.

And my father! she thought, shocked that she had not considered it before. He is still alive. I do have a place to go: my father's side.

But he would not want her. Surrounded by soldiers, he would want to die a soldier. The sobbing of his little girl would only prove how completely he had failed. Mary could do but one thing for her father: Stay away.

She reached the summit of a long, slow hill, and there on the next hill sat Inverness. Such a beautiful castle! The home to which her own father had bound her.

Mary prayed to Saint Hilda and Saint Margaret: *Whatever comes upon me, let me follow the example of my lady Macbeth. Let me be strong and good.*

Things have been strangely borne.
ACT III, SCENE 6

THERE SHE IS," SAID ILDRED. "LOOK AT HER SITTING UP ON THE meadow, Little Mistress Laziness, when we have to prepare for the King. Of course *she's* not going to help. Go get her, Swin."

Swin had no more time to fetch Lady Mary than anybody else, but she didn't mind stepping away from the heat of her cook fires. She hiked toward Lady Mary, waving and calling. Lady Mary just sat there, which did not endear her to Swin. "Where have you been?" Swin shouted, annoyed that she was going to have to walk all the way.

"On the heath," said Mary, as if Swin should have known.

Swin could think of nothing more dangerous for pretty little

Mary than to wander where soldiers were crawling all over the place. "What do you mean – on the heath?"

"I followed you."

Lady Mary knew where Swin had gone? Found the hut? Seen the stolen food?

Swin played dumb. "You never followed me anywhere. I been here all day, working the kitchens. There's a feast tomorrow, Lady Mary, to celebrate."

Lady Mary looked as stupid as a sheep. "Celebrate?"

"We won. Men been coming from the battlefield all day, and even brought Lady Macbeth a letter. Good King Duncan is safe, the princes are safe, the kingdom is safe," said Swin, silently adding, *Please God, let me be safe.*

If this caused rejoicing, Lady Mary didn't show it. She stood up only when Swin pulled her by the hand. "Lord Macbeth is back?" she asked nervously.

"Not yet. He escorts the King, I think. Look at you shivering. It's because you went out on the moor. It scares a body."

"I only did what you did, Swin. I found the Weird Ones. I thought they had you. They had something."

Swin's bones hurt. "They did evil to you, Lady Mary?"

"No. But they said –"

Swin made a cross with her index fingers and pressed it against Mary's lips to keep her from repeating whatever the witches had said. Swin looked around, but there was no sign of the un-see-able. She lowered her voice anyway. "Witches *do* help them as God won't, but you're damned if you listen, Lady Mary. Witches poke you full of truth and untruth. You can't even tell which *is* the truth, because the devil crawls through the poke-holes."

Swin hustled Lady Mary into the castle. If Lady Mary told anyone that she had followed Swin onto the moor, Swin would just shake her head and laugh it off.

"Swin," said Lady Mary, "what does it mean if your thumbs prick?"

Swin leaped away from her. Lady Mary really had found the Weird Ones. Swin crossed her fingers to ward off the power of it. "When there's pricking of the thumbs," she said, "something wicked this way comes."

I think, but dare not speak.
ACT V, SCENE 1

MARY CREPT INTO THE SOLAR LIKE A DOG EXPECTING TO be kicked.

Ildred was undoing Lady Macbeth's hair, which had been woven around a circlet of gold. The necklace worn that day had been tossed on the fat feather bed. Embroidery spilled off a bench, a book lay open, flowers tilted in a jar. It was a lovely place and a lovely hour, and Mary did not deserve it. I must tell her who I am, thought Mary. Daughter of a traitor.

Humiliation drowned her, filling her lungs. Mary thought, They will not need to execute me; I will die of shame.

Lady Macbeth picked up a folded page. It must be the letter

Swin had mentioned. Mary had never seen one, either. Ildred tried to read the words over Lady Macbeth's shoulder. Mary tried to read Lady Macbeth's expression. She owns my castle now, my lands, and my future. Does she know? What will she do with them and me?

Mary had a sick feathery feeling, as if she had turned to dust and would be swept away and burned with the trash.

A tiny smile changed the set of Lady Macbeth's lips, an odd inhuman smile; the brindled cat of the witches was in that smile. Mary closed her eyes and when she opened them, Lady Macbeth was kissing her letter.

If Asleif had ever written to Mary, she would have kissed his letter. Asleif had not been able to read or write. I would have been the perfect wife for him, she thought. I would have run our castle and handled the accounts and written the letters.

She imagined herself at Gledstane — where she would never go. With Asleif — whom she would never see again. Writing letters.

"Lady Mary," said Lady Macbeth, as if they had not met before.

Mary curtsied.

"Ildred, be sure Lady Mary looks lovely for the feast tomorrow. Dress her in my green gown, the one that looks like a forest in winter."

Mary knew the gown. Mysterious deep green like fir trees, trimmed with black fur, cut low to display a fine jewel on a slender neck. How kind of Lady Macbeth, to be generous in the midst of so many concerns. Mary must tell her the truth of things. Lady Macbeth must not be ambushed in public when it was reported that she had been nourishing a viper.

Would they think of Mary that way?

As poison? As a snake?

"And of course her hair must also be beautiful, Ildred. You will braid Lady Mary's hair in a circle, like a crown. I love crowns. Do you remember playing king and queen, Mary, when you were a little girl?" She didn't look to see if Mary remembered. "Tomorrow night, the King will come," she said to her reflection in the mirror.

Ildred set down the circlet and brushed Lady Macbeth's long, shiny hair, so black and thick. Lady Macbeth whispered to her letter. "Come, you spirits. Fill me. *I will have that golden round.*"

Mary's thumbs pricked.

"Do you mean the circlet, my lady?" said Ildred. "I put it on the dressing table."

Witches' cries filled Mary's ears. Even with her hands pressed against her head she could not escape their noise. *All hail, Macbeth, who wilt be king hereafter.*

Lady Macbeth turned very slowly on her stool. She did not glance at Ildred. She fixed her eyes on Mary. She knows and won't say, thought Mary. I have to say it first. Out loud. My father is the traitor.

I cannot!

If only I had left for Shiel, where the well is holy, where pilgrims come, and saints drink. I could be safe by now.

"It is late, Mary," said Lady Macbeth. "You must sleep. So must I. For tomorrow at the banquet we must look up clear. To alter favor is to fear."

The rhyme was disturbing, like a pebble thrown into quiet water. Mary wondered what it meant. She stared out the solar window. Only sky and stone were visible, as from a prison tower. Perhaps this was what her father saw out his window, if he had a window. Or had they tied him to a stake, leaving him out in the weather so he would know where his bones would lie? Not in a consecrated grave. Flung on the rocks, meat for foxes.

I ought to hate my father, she thought, for forcing me to bear his betrayal. But no matter what he did, I love him.

And no matter what I do – or don't do – there is no one left on earth now who loves me.

Lady Macbeth walked out of the room, holding her letter like a bouquet.

When she was gone, Ildred said, "I could kick you downstairs, Lady Mary. It isn't enough that I'm her maid instead of her companion? Now I have to be your maid as well? Why did you let Aelgitha go, anyway?"

Aelgitha! thought Mary. She knew. Fergus must have known. All my father's men must have known! Fergus came for his mother, to get her out of harm's way. Why didn't someone get me out of harm's way?

If only she could get to Shiel. . . .

Everybody knew that if you prayed three times at the well of Shiel, and three times crossed yourself with fingers dipped in holy water, it would mend you or end you.

And that was the question, of course. Would Mary be ended or mended?

Hang out our banners on the outward walls.

ACT V, SCENE 5

I
T WAS NOT UNTIL MIDAFTERNOON THE NEXT DAY THAT THEY FIRST SAW the bright distant colors of King Duncan and his victorious men, marching toward the castle.

From the walls of Inverness came one shout from one throat, and then hundreds of cheers. The King was coming. Even the swallows celebrated, swooping back and forth like tiny excited flags.

It was wrong for Mary to be in the presence of the very king her father had hoped to dethrone, but she could not miss the sight of a real true king any more than the stable boys or Swin or Ildred could. She hid herself behind flapping banners on a tower and drank in the glory of the procession. Duncan was magnificent. His armor gleamed, his white hair shone, his massive black horse stepped high. He carried no weapons, of course, because his lords rode at his side. What shame would attach to their names if they could not protect his sacred self.

At this moment, all shame attached to Mary. King Duncan did not know her. Perhaps he did not even know *about* her; soldiers did not talk of their daughters. But many did know, and soon, all of them would.

"Honored hostess," called Duncan, his voice carrying over the crowd, "how pleasant is the seat of your castle."

The people murmured with delight: They were part of a castle pleasing to a king. Even Swin stood more proud. But not Ildred; she was never pleased with anything.

"Your majesty, you honor our house," replied Lady Macbeth. "I welcome you. We have been praying for you. Now it is our privilege to house you."

"Fair and noble lady," said the King, "give me your hand."

So this was how kings talked! And that was how a lady answered. Unless of course the lady was Mary – a traitor's daughter. *Then* how did she answer a king?

"And where," said the King, lifting his voice to be heard by the most distant deaf old farmer, "is the new Thane of Cawdor?"

No one spoke, because no one knew what he meant. Even from Lady Macbeth there was silence. But she knows, thought Mary. The letter must have told her about it.

Lady Macbeth simply waited. She wants the King to make the announcement, thought Mary. It's more important that way.

"Cawdor was my enemy, yet I had no inkling," Duncan said, raising his voice for the crowd. "He joined Macdonwald, and both these men betrayed me. But Cawdor was caught. And so to Macbeth, my valiant cousin, I have given Cawdor's title."

The crowd took his meaning: All that wealth and land now belonged to Lord and Lady Macbeth and the splendid castle also. And none of it was Mary's.

Lady Macbeth acted as if she cared nothing for honors and increase. Instead she repeated the King's question. "Where is my husband, sire?" She smiled. "A man with the great privilege of having you in his home has work to do."

The King laughed. "I am sure, dear lady, that you have accomplished all that needs doing and always will."

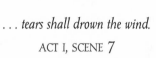

. . . tears shall drown the wind.
ACT I, SCENE 7

ILDRED WATCHED AS MARY DOUBLED OVER AS IF STABBED IN THE GUT and ran to hide in her room. So that was why Mary had to look lovely at the feast – she would face the King and be told her fate. Beauty would add to the excitement.

Had Mary known? Probably not. Mary didn't have the brains God gave a goose. But I bet Aelgitha knew, thought Ildred. That's why her son saved her.

Oh, to have a son who grew up to save you. Or even a son who grew up.

The King and his men entered the courtyard, and the people, satisfied with their glimpse of glory, dispersed. They would be fed at the scullery door – thick slabs of brown bread with meat drippings and onions.

The King of Scotland gave his horse to a groom and strode toward the hall with his officers by his side.

Lady Macbeth climbed the stairs to her room, thus leaving the King without host or hostess. And when Lord Macbeth arrived shortly after, springing from his horse, he took the steps two at a time to see his wife, not his king. Ildred was not surprised. She had seldom seen a man and woman so tightly bound.

Dirle strained at his leash to follow Swin into the kitchen. No matter how much Ildred tried to convince herself that Dirle loved her, he always wanted a bone more.

In the kitchen, they were talking of traitors and whether Lady Mary would be allowed to live. The moment Ildred came in, Swin changed the subject. She was always doing that. It hurt.

"I heard Father Ninian buried that baby," said Swin.

"The one found in the ditch?" asked Rousay. "Lady Macbeth said it couldn't get buried, not some dead thing born to some drab."

"Father Ninian says the Lord loves every sparrow that falls," said Swin. "I don't think he buried it in the churchyard, but he did bless it. Even wrapped it in a beautiful white cloth with white lace. An old altar cloth maybe."

Fhiora was irked. "*I* don't have lace. Why does some bastard baby get it?"

"Did you see the lace on the King's sleeves?" asked Rousay. "Wasn't it beautiful?"

Swin harped on the baby. "Father Ninian says it's right to give the baby one good thing, one good moment, one good prayer."

"Since when do you care what Father Ninian says?" Jennet wanted to know.

"I heard the witches got at that babe," said Fhiora.

"No," said Swin. "Or Father Ninian would have said."

"But —" said Fhiora.

Swin kicked her. Fhiora kicked back. Swin smacked her. Fhiora smacked back.

"Is this how you behave when the King of Scotland is under our roof?" demanded Ildred.

Swin turned her beaky stare on Ildred. "Going to tell him?"

No, thought Ildred. I'm not telling anybody anything.

She sat in a corner, heavy with secrets, and watched them work.

⁂

Why do you dress me
In borrowed robes?
ACT I, SCENE 3

⁂

MARY DIDN'T BOTHER TO SHUT HER DOOR BEHIND HER — she couldn't hide from the truth. She was startled to see spread out on her bed the gown chosen for her to wear tonight. Mary held it up. It was long, but that would give her something to do — lifting the front skirt of the gown to keep from tripping. It looked wide in the shoulders, too, so she'd have to keep hers very straight. Maybe posture would give her courage.

She heard Lord Macbeth charging up the stairs, heedless of everything but his wife. *Oh, Asleif. I will never have that with you.*

Mary knew just how they were looking at each other, the way they always did, full of secrets. Then came Lady Macbeth's voice, rich with pride and full of teasing. "You fought that traitor Macdonwald," she said to her husband.

He was laughing the way he had on the moor. "Sword to sword. Did you like my letter?"

"A fine piece of news. You curbed his lavish spirit."

Indeed, Macdonwald had been lavish with everything, throwing around money and flair and courage. Now he had squandered his life. Mary's father had been like that, too. Big and noisy, generous and loud – splurging his gold, his strength, his hopes. And now Mary.

Let your remembrance apply to Banquo . . .
ACT III, SCENE 2

I F KING DUNCAN HAD MADE MACBETH THE THANE OF CAWDOR, WHAT great gift of power would go to his father, Banquo? Fleance could hardly wait to hear. From his table – a fine seat close to the dais – Fleance drank in the sight of his own father sitting next to the King. Lady Macbeth was on Duncan's other side, while Lord Macbeth came and went, as hosts do.

Fleance envied how the Macbeths looked at each other: bedroom looks. Fleance had no experience in that direction. He wondered what Seyton had done last night and with whom. Far away, at one of the lower tables, Seyton caught his eye and grinned again. Even at this distance, the grin gripped Fleance in the gut and twisted it. He had left things too late. There was no rescuing honor now. He would always live a lie.

Fleance watched the two princes. Malcolm drank from a horn, tipping the curly end to his mouth and swigging without spilling a drop. Donalbain drank straight from the bowl, slurping and laughing and wiping his mouth with his sleeve. Both appealed to Fleance. The casual artistry of the drinking horn was princely, but the careless spill from the bowl was manly.

"I begin now," said King Duncan, "to honor those who have served me so well." He started with Macbeth, which he had to do, since this was Macbeth's castle. "Valiant cousin, your new title: Thane of Cawdor."

"To be in your service is payment enough, sire," said Macbeth, although every man present knew perfectly well it was *not* payment enough. But courtesy came first and then treasure. All over the room, men gossiped about Cawdor.

Duncan motioned for silence.

This is it, thought Fleance. This is when Duncan gives my father a castle and new titles and land.

"All who are near and dear to us," said the King, "hear now our decision."

Fleance loved the royal we. A king was Power personified, both man and throne, and his speech must reflect it.

"We will now name our heir," said the King, and Fleance's eyes flew open. "Our older son, Malcolm, is your future king."

Do you not hope your children shall be kings...
ACT I, SCENE 3

S EYTON WAS STUNNED.

Duncan had chosen *Malcolm?*

Seyton would have expected one of the two brilliant generals: Banquo or Macbeth.

In an instant, everything changed. It was now Prince Malcolm who would one day be Seyton's king.

Usually a king in Scotland was chosen, at least in part, by acclamation. Since Duncan had bypassed the custom, his men provided it. They leaped to their feet, clapping and stomping and cheering. Up came the tankards, cups, and mugs, as every man raised a glass to Prince Malcolm.

Seyton looked to see how his lord was taking this.

Lord Macbeth was not looking at Prince Malcolm. Not even looking at King Duncan. He was staring at Banquo.

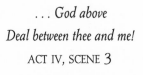

. . . God above
Deal between thee and me!
ACT IV, SCENE 3

F ATHER NINIAN WAS GENTLE. "YOU HEARD WHAT I SAID, ILDRED.
Say a Pater Noster for Lady Mary and be a friend to her."

"A friend to Mary!" cried Ildred, who was not going to
say the Our Father for her. "I despise Mary!"

"Love her," said Father Ninian.

"Impossible!"

"Nothing is impossible with God at your side," said Father
Ninian. "God will walk with you, and you will walk with Mary.
It will not be a long walk, I suspect. Nor will it be required of you
for more than a day or two. Lady Macbeth has ordered Lady
Mary to be at this banquet, and you will stay by her side."

. . . weary with disasters, tugged with fortune . . .
ACT III, SCENE 1

M ARY STOOD LIKE A STICK INSIDE THE HEAVY FOLDS OF LADY
Macbeth's green gown. Ildred had woven her hair
at the very top of her head so not a wisp touched

her neck. No jewel lay at her throat, and the gown scooped low both in front and in back. It was a dress to be executed in.

She couldn't go in there, she couldn't.

Every man in this hall had lifted his sword against Cawdor and Cawdor against them. Every man in this hall had heard the King address Macbeth by Mary's father's title. Every man knew Mary's father was to die a traitor's death.

The guests had entered the hall by its large double main doors, but Ildred and Mary lingered at the back, where a short stone hall connected it to the kitchen, providing some hope that were there a kitchen fire, it could be contained.

Mary would not have thought so many could be seated in this room. It was very crowded. Lady Macbeth wanted a greater hall, where the head table was permanent. She would have it at Cawdor, which was a finer castle.

The men were boisterous and loud from the proclamation of Malcolm as heir. All eyes were on the princes.

Ildred went in. Mary followed. In that great gathering, Ildred alone wore sad, plain clothing, dark as mourning. Amidst the revelers in yellow and cobalt blue, emerald green and bloodred, amidst plaid and stripe and embroidery, Ildred looked ready for her coffin.

Mary's skirt was very full. It caught on table edges and brushed elbows. Men grew silent as she passed. When she took a breath, her lungs stuck, as if they did not want more air; they wanted her to die and be done with it.

At last they reached a bench with space. Ildred slid in. Mary lowered herself onto the outer few inches, perching like a bird.

Except a bird had all heaven to fly in, and Mary had nowhere. The men across from her stiffened but did not leave, although Mary's father had perhaps killed their brothers or fathers and had certainly killed their kerns.

Two knights entered the hall. Not from the kitchen, where Mary had crept in, but from the great doors that opened to the forecourt. Duncan gave them permission to speak.

"My lord," said the first, shouting the glad tidings, "Cawdor has been hanged."

CHAPTER 4

Come what come may,
Time and the hour runs through the roughest day.

ACT I, SCENE 3

SOMETIMES A CRIMINAL'S DEEDS WERE SO DIRE THAT THE NEIGHBORS wanted to stone him. They would bury the criminal alive under stones instead of hanging him – or her – by the neck. Each glare in this vast hall was a stone crushing Mary's chest. Her eyes glazed over, and she saw only color and wrath.

"Cawdor confessed," said the second knight. "Then we put the rope around his neck and shoved him off."

My father, thought Mary.

"Cawdor begged for your majesty's pardon," the knights told King Duncan.

Mary did not believe this. She had never heard her father say he was sorry. He would have been sorry only because he lost. To her amazement, the knights then praised her father. "Nothing in his life was as noble as how he left it. Cawdor died as if he had rehearsed."

Mary imagined him in his cell, practicing for his own execution. She gripped the table edge to keep from fainting.

The King spoke so mildly that Mary thought he had already lost interest. "Cawdor deceived me well. I built my trust on him and never suspected. It is a lesson to us all. The thoughts of a man are not visible in his face."

Mary struggled to keep her own thoughts invisible but failed. Tears spilled. She could not let go of the table to wipe them away.

There was no more discussion of Cawdor. Whatever place her father had held in any heart but hers, he was dead now and didn't matter. How he would have hated that.

Men had battle stories to share, and they talked of bloodshed and honor and loot. Many names were mentioned. Asleif's was not one. The name spoken most often was Malcolm's. The King could not get enough of saying, "My son Malcolm will be the king of his generation."

"King hereafter!" came the toast.

She heard again the witches' cry. *Macbeth, who shall be king hereafter.* Had her father thought *he* would be king hereafter? Or had Cawdor planned to put the King of Norway on the throne of Scotland?

Macbeth, who shall be king hereafter.

Out on the moor, Macbeth had laughed at this prophecy.

Perhaps he thought the Weird Ones were just hungry old things hoping for a coin. And yet...they had known Macbeth was going to become Cawdor *before* Ross and Lennox arrived to announce it. What if the Weird Ones were right about everything they prophesied? Impossible. What dread events would bump the crown from Duncan to Malcolm to Macbeth?

But Macbeth did not seem to be watching glamorous young Malcolm or to be thinking that he was supposed to be king hereafter. Macbeth did not even seem interested in his own banquet. He kept drifting out of the hall. More than once, Lady Macbeth also eased away from the high table and went to her husband's side. This was not unusual. He was always seeking her advice, and she was constantly lifting his heart.

Not once did either of them glance at Mary. She was almost offended. Lord and Lady Macbeth had just become rich and powerful while she had just become poor and powerless. Didn't they want to show pity – or gloat? To be kind – or judge? If nothing more, Mary and Ildred were the only other women there, because men did not take their wives to war. Mary would have thought that their gowns alone would draw Lady Macbeth's eye. No.

But to everyone else, Mary was of great interest. Courtesy kept her safe. Courtesy was crucial among thanes; no one would tease or torment. But as the evening wore on, Mary saw that courtesy had nothing to do with it: They were eying her as Swin eyed a flock of geese. Which was the fattest?

I am like the kerns, she thought. I am livestock.

Men would not bid for love. They were not planning to adorn

her with jewels. They didn't care about making a home or having babies. Men would bid to own Shiel, its glen and its river, and all the deer and timber and rents therein.

She was grateful that no one seemed to be thinking of executing her. But marriage, which had meant Asleif and true love and a home at Gledstane – these were lost.

There were possibilities other than marriage. Lord and Lady Macbeth might do nothing and, to all intents and purposes, just own Shiel. Mary would be lower than Ildred.

Or they could put her in a nunnery and wed her to God, giving her the smallest possible dowry – just her share of the convent maintenance – and keeping the rest. Mary loved the Lord. She would serve the Lord with gladness, but she wanted Asleif.

Dear Lord, let Asleif be alive. Let him be safe in Norway. Let him come for me.

... my more-having would be as a sauce
To make me hunger more ...
ACT IV, SCENE 3

SWIN WAS SERVING, WHICH SHE RARELY DID. HER TASK WAS THE kitchen, where she would be spattered with grease and dripping with sweat and not fit to carry trays among the guests. But the castle was stretched to feed so many, and some servants had died in battle or been wounded.

King and princes, lords and thanes – and Lady Mary, tossed from her life like a broken dory on the sand, stranded among her father's enemies. Next to her sat Ildred, pretending to be a friend.

Just wants Lady Mary's room, thought Swin, forgetting pity.

Where was Dirle? Several dogs were wandering around – not the savage hunting dogs, which had always to be chained up – but the pets of officers. The men – typical – were throwing their dogs rich fatty scraps that any peasant standing at the door would gladly have devoured.

The lords all looked alike to Swin. Lennox and Ross, Angus and Menteith, Caithness, Macduff, and Banquo – who could tell?

No matter where she went, her lord Macbeth was in the way. What was the matter with the man? The King of Scotland was his guest – and Macbeth had better things to do? Nothing needed fixing. Everybody was doing their best. They all wanted to impress the King.

And then it was *Lady* Macbeth wandering around and getting in Swin's way.

Lady Macbeth neither saw nor heard her. And what was more, the lady did not notice *Mary*, from whose family she had just acquired a new title and a new castle.

Again and again the King shouted, "My son Malcolm!" and so forth, and smack down on the table went the cups as the men drummed for joy. Swin thought gloomily of the cleanup.

It seemed to Swin that a good king would name his successor prior to the battle. What if Duncan had gone into that battle and gotten himself killed? Then his open throne would have led to yet another war while everybody struggled to get the power for himself.

Well, of course, men talked about their own dying only when there was no chance of it. Everybody here had lived through the fight, so they liked talking about death. Yelling their battle stories, every soldier made it sound as if he had killed his ten thousands, like David in the Bible. There probably weren't that many men in Norway to start with.

No matter how exciting the stories, though, some men were not listening. They were too busy eyeing Lady Mary. She was young, beautiful, innocent, and no longer betrothed. That man of hers was dead somewhere on the sand or had run to Norway. Didn't count anyway. Mary was property.

They were all wondering whether to bid.

Come, love and health to all!
ACT III, SCENE 4

ILDRED FELT AS IF FOXES WERE CHEWING ON HER HEART.

She was one of only three women in this huge hall. Many of these men were widowed and could take a wife. Many had a son, a nephew, or a cousin in need of a wife. Here sat Ildred, who came from a good family and had good blood and not one man looked at her and thought of her for wifehood. They looked at Mary.

Mary sat motionless. She neither ate nor drank. Probably choke or drown if she did.

I'd choke you in a minute, thought Ildred. How dare you? Your

father a traitor, your betrothed fighting against these very men —
and still you attract eyes and I don't.

Ildred fixed her gaze on lords with sons. She stared at Lord
Macduff, all of whose children were babies, but who had a
cousin. He never glanced at her. She stared at Ross, who had two
younger brothers. Ross never glanced at her.

How feverish were Lady Macbeth's eyes. Ildred knew that glitter, those eyes that always wanted more. But what more could
there possibly be?

. . . sleep that knits up the raveled sleave of care . . .
ACT II, SCENE 2

FLEANCE WAS DESPERATE FOR SLEEP, BUT NOBODY COULD LEAVE THE
table until the King did, and Duncan acted as if he might
celebrate for days. Pages curled up on rushes and went to
sleep on the floor. Knights put their heads down on the table
and snored into their food. Fleance propped his chin in his hand.
Finally, Lady Macbeth coaxed the King to rise. All stood to honor
his departure, some more shakily than others — there had been
many toasts to Malcolm.

A shimmer of auburn hair and green gown drew Fleance's
eyes. He had forgotten that Lady Mary existed. Actually, right
now, she hardly did. He wondered if she was still Lady Mary of
Shiel or whether Shiel and its title also went to the new Thane
of Cawdor. Lady Mary was fortunate in one thing: She was

lovely in a pale, frozen way, and some man might want to warm her up.

Lady Macbeth was assigning places to sleep, insuring that high-ranking men had comfortable spots and that every warrior at least got clean straw under a roof, either here or in the stables. The King and his two body servants would sleep in the Macbeths' own chamber, she announced, while the princes would share a small but fine bedroom adjacent to their father. Lord Menteith was to sleep here and Lord Lennox there; Caithness and Angus in this room and Macduff in that.

Banquo caught his son's eye and nodded toward the courtyard, and Fleance understood that he was to meet his father. He hoped he could totter that far.

Some young officer suddenly sprang forward, knelt before Prince Malcolm, and in ringing tones, swore his loyalty. When the day came – although, please God, King Duncan would be well and wise for years to come – but when the day came, his sword and heart belonged to Malcolm.

The beauty of this declaration gave them zest again, and they lined up for the privilege of kneeling before their future king.

Yet my heart
Throbs to know one thing.
ACT IV, SCENE 1

MARY HAD NOT BEEN ABLE TO SPEAK AND NOW COULD NOT move. When Ildred rose to acknowledge the King's departure, Mary couldn't remember how to stand. Ildred glared; the whole room glared. Now the traitor's daughter was so disrespectful she lounged while the King was on his feet.

Mary hauled herself up by the table edge.

The only small but fine bedroom adjacent to Lady Macbeth's chamber was Mary's. The princes had been given her room.

The walk out of the hall seemed like a trek over mountains. And what was the point? Mary had nowhere to go. Her little felt slippers poked rhythmically out from under the fir-green hem, moving – moving – toward what?

She felt eyes.

Somebody looking at her so hard that he saw her naked body and the babies he would get on her and the rents and castles he would own through her.

Her thumbs pricked.

The room was chaos – Lady Macbeth shepherding people one way, Lord Macbeth taking a crowd out another door, thanes escorting the King, young men lining up before Malcolm, servants clearing tables, dogs eating bones.

But the eyes stayed on Mary. She stopped walking. Slowly, she turned, searching for the man stripping her of clothing and hope. They all were.

<hr />

There's husbandry in heaven;
Their candles are all out.
ACT II, SCENE 1

<hr />

N OT ONE STAR TONIGHT," SAID BANQUO. HE SOUNDED VERY TIRED. "Here, Fleance. Take my sword. My dirk as well."

Fleance loved being his father's page, but he was startled. Why was his father armed? They were safe inside the walls of Inverness. The King's men strewed the ground like rushes. In the towers, watchmen paced for no reason Fleance could see. Who would approach? The enemy was vanquished.

A servant boy appeared with a torch. Its light flickered on Banquo, and Fleance saw lines of worry. "I can't settle my heart," said his father. "I dread sleep. I fear my own dreams."

Fleance was rattled. He didn't want to dream about Brude, but he had not thought his father would mind a battle or two.

There was a sound in the dark, nothing meaningful, yet Banquo yanked Fleance to his side, demanding of the night, "Who's there?" And then, his voice so low even the torch boy could not hear, he said to Fleance, "Give me back the sword" – and snatched it before Fleance could present it.

The torch boy swung his light to reveal Lord Macbeth, who was chuckling. "Just a friend," teased their host.

Behind their bodies, deep in shadow, Banquo returned the sword to Fleance, who lined it up behind his leg so it wouldn't be seen. It was embarrassing to be holding a weapon, as if they didn't think their host could take care of them.

"While you and your lady were getting the men settled, I got Duncan safely down," said Banquo.

Fleance was embarrassed again. Of course King Duncan was safe.

The two captains shared a smile. No one had enjoyed this banquet as much as Duncan himself. The evening was a triumph for Lady Macbeth.

Banquo held out his hand. "The King gave me something for you," he said to Macbeth. "Actually, for your lady. In the excitement, Duncan forgot to present it to her." In Banquo's palm glittered a gem so bright Fleance thought perhaps the sky was free of stars because they had collected in this diamond.

Even more for Macbeth? thought Fleance. But what about my father?

Involuntarily, his fingers shifted on the sword handle. How quickly jealousy could run down a man's arm and out the tip of his weapon.

Macbeth hardly glanced at the diamond, just took it and forgot it.

The torch flickered and went out.

Some bird cried, over and over, like a baby abandoned.

"I had a dream last night," said Banquo, "about the Weird Ones we met."

Lord Macbeth and Fleance's father had consulted witches? This seemed extraordinary to Fleance. They were men of action, not prophecy.

"I haven't had time to think about that," said Macbeth. "We should talk, though."

His father's voice was strained. "To you they showed some truth."

"Stay with me," said Macbeth, "and there will be honors."

There was a pause. "If," said Banquo slowly, "my heart is clear about it."

They bowed to each other.

"Good repose," said Macbeth, as if it were a dare.

Good things of day begin to droop and drowse . . .
ACT III, SCENE 2

WIN LIT NEITHER CANDLE NOR LANTERN IN THE KITCHEN. IT WAS SO hot in there already, and the light of the cook fires was enough. But now the fires dwindled into piles of red winking eyes, and the great kitchen was all shadow. She carried out the ashes, setting them aside for making soap another day. She threw the vegetable peels to the geese. She brought in firewood for the morning.

In the Great Hall, the menservants were stacking the benches and tables against the walls, a noisy undertaking, and one that required persuading the drunken guests to move.

Swin tossed a great bone into the pot and scraped in leftover gravy and bread, baked fruit and onions. In the morning she would boil barley and the soup would be a feast for those with appetite to think of food. Those who had had too much to drink and those whose lives were over, like Lady Mary, would not be among them.

Lady Macbeth swept in, carrying her own candle in a pierced metal cylinder. Her hand was visible around the candle, but the rest of her was vague, like dreams in the dark. Her crimson gown looked like poured blood. Her gold embroidered headpiece glittered like a crown.

Swin was astonished to see the mistress in this slop and stink. She curtsied awkwardly.

"To bed," ordered Lady Macbeth.

"My lady," protested Swin, "we haven't even gotten all the food out of the hall." She glimpsed Lady Mary also creeping into the kitchen, slippers silent on the stones. The girl merged with the shadows as she dropped her face into her hands and vanished like a ghost in the night.

Lady Macbeth did not see her. "Quickly then," said the lady. "The King is tired. He must be abed and undisturbed by noise."

The kitchen staff had nothing to do with bed; they did not enter the upper chambers. Such rooms were kept clean, and people like Swin were not clean. Swin figured that after a war and all those toasts, the King would sleep like the dead. He wouldn't hear if the chimney came down.

Lady Macbeth did not see Swin hang a haunch of untouched beef on a ceiling hook, nor Jennet stacking trays, nor Fhiora sanding out pots. She held her right hand up to the dim shivery light of her candle and studied it. Then she traded hands and studied her left. In a whisper light as a breath, Lady Macbeth spoke as if the servants were not there — as if nobody was there, not even God, who heard everything. "These are hangman's hands," she murmured, as if this made her proud.

Present fears
Are less than horrible imaginings . . .
ACT I, SCENE 3

ARY HUDDLED IN THE DARK, AS MUCH A PART OF THE KITCHEN as a pot or a bowl. She wanted to fling herself on Lady Macbeth's mercy.

I didn't mean for this to happen, she would cry. I didn't know what my father was doing. I don't know where to sleep tonight or what will become of me.

But Lady Macbeth was not motherly and would not offer comfort. Indeed, she seemed astonished that the staff still had work, as if she had forgotten what scullery maids did.

Scullery. An ugly word for an ugly room — where Swin killed geese, for example, dipped them in boiling water, removed the feathers, and cut off the feet for the dogs to eat. The meat itself went into the kitchen. *Kitchen* was a good word, warm and welcoming.

To insult a man, you called him a slave. To insult a woman, you called her a scullion.

I can face what is to come if I just *know*, thought Mary. Is it marriage? Is it death? Is it the nunnery?

The thought entered her mind that she could go back to the Weird Ones; they would know.

These are hangman's hands, said someone or something.

Her thumbs pricked.

Was that said by Swin, who executed the beasts of the field? Duncan, who had executed her father? Soldiers, who executed one another?

"The princes sleep in Lady Mary's chamber," said Lady Macbeth to Swin. "She can sleep with you tonight."

Mary stared at her thumbs.

She did not have to go to witches to learn the future. She had just been told. She would be a scullery maid.

<hr>

> *. . . we'll drink a measure*
> *The table round.*
> ACT III, SCENE 4

<hr>

AND A POT TO PISS IN," ORDERED THE KING'S BODY SERVANT.
Ildred hated him. She was not a chambermaid who handled chamber pots! But she got it for him.

"And a jug of water," ordered the other body servant.

Ildred hated him, too. She got the jug of water. She could not believe that only two men were to sleep in the solar. There was space for a dozen here. Even though Ildred hated having to sleep here in the solar on a cot, she was furious to be put out for a couple of stupid, arrogant servants. There were thanes sleeping two to a mattress in the hall! Officers and gentlemen could be in this delightful space. Who were these servants to –

There was a knock. "Yes?" snapped Ildred.

"I have some very fine wine for the King's servants," said Lady Macbeth, ignoring Ildred as usual but smiling at the men and bringing forward a great tankard. "You have done outstanding work and need a reward."

This was news to Ildred. She had done it all. What on earth was Lady Macbeth doing here? Ildred had fixed the north chamber for Lord and Lady Macbeth, the one over the chapel.

Lady Macbeth poured each man his own cup and one for herself. "Go to bed, Ildred," she said without looking. "Find a place in the stable with Mary. Plenty of straw."

These servants were going to stay up drinking with Lady Macbeth, and Ildred got straw? The rage that usually drove Ildred failed her. She dragged herself down the stairs and toward the stable.

She found straw. She did not find Lady Mary, and she did not find Dirle. She had to have her dog. She had to cling to him and convince herself that at least Dirle loved her.

Nor heaven peep through the blanket of the dark
to cry "Hold, hold!"
ACT I, SCENE 5

WHEN LADY MACBETH LEFT THE KITCHEN, THE COALS ON THE hearth flared up by themselves, like devils peeking through. Mary kept her eyes on the fire in case they stepped out. She impaled a fresh tallow candle on the spike of a candlestick and left the kitchen, picking her way across the open courtyard, where animals and men slept in huddles, using one another for pillows and warmth.

The chapel was blacker than night and more empty. It even felt empty of God. Mary needed to pray for her father's soul, but she could find neither words nor hope. She knelt. Wind slammed the chapel door and put out her candle.

The dark was so dark she couldn't bear it. She closed her eyes, hiding inside herself. But apparently she was not really hidden, because she could feel something looking at her.

Not God.

Not His saints.

She turned her cheek on the cold stone floor and looked.

A dead-light, its bones visible under its dead skin, shivered with malice just inside the door. She should have known. They always put out candles.

The dead-light spoke. *"Glamis thou are, and now Cawdor."*

Mary blinked. It was just Lady Macbeth, whispering as she had in the kitchen. "And," the lady added, "you shall be more. You shall be everything the witches promised."

The perfectly ordinary voice of Lord Macbeth said, "We will proceed no further. He has honored me. I'm his cousin. His virtues stand by him like angels, can't you see that? And in his glory I stand."

"Reflected glory?" said Lady Macbeth sharply. "That's what we live for? I think not. Would you live a coward?"

Mary bit down on her thumb to press out the pricking.

"What if we fail?" said Macbeth.

Lady Macbeth was disgusted. "Screw your courage to the sticking place."

If they saw Mary, they would know her for a spy, like her father before her. Why had she not gone into the stable the way she had been told? Because she thought herself too good for obedience, also like her father – and like him, she would meet some dread end. Mary tried to screw her own courage to the sticking place.

"Bring forth men children only," said Macbeth, his voice shaking.

What could make the voice of great Macbeth tremble?

His wife's speech was slow and lingering. "Great Glamis, worthy Cawdor, dearest love. Our future is this instant."

The shaking was love, then, not fear. The heat of their passion was so intense Mary felt herself melt from it. She blushed to think what they were going to do in this instant to which Lady

Macbeth referred. But they did not stay in the chapel, and neither did Mary.

She yearned to do something right, and the only choice was to obey that order and sleep in the stable. She got as far as the barn door. The gloom of night rose thick and yeasty around her. If Mary walked into that barn and lay down with the animals, she was admitting that straw was good enough for her.

"Lady Mary?"

She jumped, but it was just Lord Macbeth's squire, Seyton. "I didn't mean to frighten you," he said softly. "I'm checking on our horses. I'm sorry for your loss, Lady Mary. Your heart must be sore."

It was a relief to be addressed gently. So kindly did he put his hand on her shoulder. The touch shot through her, and she thought, He pities me. Pity is all I will ever have now, not love. "Once," she said, "I thought to live on an estate called Gledstane." Immediately, she regretted speaking of Asleif. Of course, Seyton didn't know Asleif existed and certainly didn't know about Gledstane.

"Ah, the old language. It will be called Gladstone soon, won't it?" said Seyton. "Even *thane* is an old word now. In the south, they are calling them earls."

Easier to think about how words changed than how lives changed.

"Is Gledstane another of your own estates?" asked Seyton.

Mary heard greed in his voice and knew that his touch was not even pity. "Good night, Seyton," she managed.

"Good night, Mhaire. " He said her name the old way, soft and hushed, like her mother in a lullabye.

She walked into the barn. She had forgotten that every lord would sleep indoors and every page at his master's side – but the lower orders would end up in the stable. She had forgotten that they would still be in a mood to celebrate, and that some celebrations required a girl – pretty or plain, willing or unwilling. The men called things to her that a day ago, they would not have dared.

She backed out, hoping to catch up to Seyton and beg him for help, which he would give for his master Macbeth's sake. But instead she bumped into Fleance, the half-grown son of Banquo. "Good evening, Lady Mary," he said delightedly.

Another greedy one. "Good evening." Mary lifted her skirts and walked faster, as if she had some idea where to go.

"I can find you a place to sleep," offered Fleance, and from the open barn door came roars of laughter and dirty jokes.

Mary managed to keep walking. Fleance walked with her, perhaps to follow up on one of the vile suggestions. He was exactly her size, which could not be pleasant for him among men. But it did mean Mary had a chance to fight him off if necessary.

They reached the scullery. Mary prayed that Swin or Jennet or Rousay or Fhiora was there. She prayed they did not all have soldiers with them.

Fleance shook out the folds of the cloak he had tossed over his shoulder in a casual boyish way, imitating the princes. He held it open, as if intending to wrap both himself and her in this one garment. Hanging from the heavy cloth was a great gold brooch.

"You took that off a body?" said Mary.

Fleance looked uneasy. "Well, sort of."

In that gold shape was every hope and dream she had ever had. Mary unpinned Asleif's brooch. She flipped it so the long, sharp pin stuck out between her fingers, and she stabbed Fleance.

CHAPTER 5

Your son, my lord, has paid a soldier's debt.
ACT V, SCENE 8

HER STAB HARDLY PUNCTURED THE CLOTH, NEVER MIND HIS HEART.
All Mary did was bend the pin.

Fleance giggled in a stupid little-boy way.

You who killed Asleif and looted his precious body – you dare laugh? thought Mary. "The man who wore this?" She spoke quietly, although she wanted to scream and weep. "I was to wed him."

Fleance stopped laughing.

The gold work on the pin was intricate, a geometry of twisted vines, like the art chiseled on stone crosses at the side of the road. Asleif deserved a cross like that on his grave. He would never have it. No one could tell Mary now what her father and her beloved had been planning, or whether they had thought of her. They were both dead.

Even after all these years, Mary could not think of her mother as that strange and absent thing – dead. Even now, Mary would find herself thinking, I'll tell Mother about this. Or, Mother will like that. The complete absence of one you loved was impossible. It was why she believed in heaven. The complete absence of those He loved would be impossible for God, too.

Now her vibrant, loud father, so full of demands, was also dead. As for Asleif – when she held his brooch in her hand, there was no escape from the truth. Asleif was dead.

"But it was war," said Fleance nervously. "He was a traitor. He would have killed the King if he could."

"No. He tried to kill you. I regret that he failed."

From the barn came a shivery moan that seemed to turn a corner and become a dying scream. Fleance fumbled for his dirk.

Mary pointed to the barn doors. "Quick! Get him!"

Fleance stepped into the shadow, dirk drawn, and Mary fled.

It was the owl that shrieked, the fatal bellman . . .
ACT II, SCENE 2

I T WAS JUST AN OWL," SAID PRINCE MALCOLM, HOLDING UP HIS TORCH to illuminate Fleance. "You almost stabbed poor Lady Ildred with that dirk."

Ildred saw Fleance's shock of humiliation. The poor boy tried to hide his embarrassment by bending his knee to Prince Malcolm, who yanked him back up. "I'm not king yet," the prince said, laughing gently.

"Sorry," mumbled Fleance. "I thought it was somebody dying or attacking."

Ildred had thought so, too, nor did she believe in the owl story. She was impressed that Fleance had had the presence of mind to attack an unearthly sound with an earthly weapon, and she was puzzled by the prince. Tonight of all nights, he was wandering unattended in barns and carrying his own torch?

"It's late," said Malcolm. "We should all be abed. Lady Ildred, have you no place to sleep but this barn? I fear we have displaced the household badly."

She had not been addressed as "Lady" for years. It was a courtesy title, anyhow, because legally only her mother could be called Lady. That the future King of Scotland would be chivalrous to Ildred almost broke her heart. She could not bear to be a trouble to him. "I'm sleeping in the kitchen," she said quickly. "It's warm there, and I have my pallet."

She didn't. It was still in the solar. Unused. Those stupid servants were being given the *couch*, as if they mattered, or were nobles in disguise.

"I'm glad," said the future king. "I thought you looked upset, though, when you walked through the barn."

Ildred's throat caught, and she feared she would sob in front of him. "I've lost my dog."

"Always worth getting upset about," agreed Malcolm. "I love my dogs."

The three of them were walking slowly toward the scullery door. Ildred must not let the prince set foot in such a lowly place.

From the barn came the shriek once more, so eerie that all three whipped around to face the evil. "It sounds like a baby," whispered Fleance. "A child thrown away."

Ildred closed her eyes.

"It's just an owl," said Malcolm stoutly. "Here, take my arm, Lady Ildred. Where have you looked for your dog?"

"Dirle is here with me, sir," said Swin, standing in the door of the scullery like a ghost. "Dogs come where meat is."

Malcolm laughed. "I like to think my dog comes because she loves me. Are you sure you'll be all right here, Lady Ildred?"

She nodded.

"Good night then. Come, Fleance. To bed." They walked away, the darkness swallowing them, and Ildred's heart went with the prince.

The mind I sway by and the heart I bear
Shall never sag with doubt nor shake with fear.
ACT V, SCENE 3

MARY WATCHED THEM COME AND GO.

In her dreams of marriage to Asleif, she had a home full of affection and the simple chores of daily life: sheep in flocks, babes in cribs, soup in bowls, sheets on lines. In only two days, Mary of Shiel, daughter of Cawdor, had become homeless. She began to see how people got so lost in life that they just stumbled out on the moor and lived there, either prey or predator. She, too, could stumble out on that moor. After all, what was left to be afraid of? What could make this worse?

I'm going to Shiel, she decided. Right now. I don't care if I'm alone. I don't care whether or not my shoes are sturdy. I don't care if I have food. I'll reach Shiel or I won't.

Hundreds of men were staying in this castle or in the fields beyond the walls. Most had had too much to drink. And before they tipped that cup there had been days of fear and one full day of battle. Tomorrow they would sleep late, and when they woke, they would think about headaches. Even on ordinary days, few noticed whether Mary was there. It might be the day after tomorrow before anybody really wondered about her and another full day before anyone bothered to look.

She would go by road. No one else would be using it. On this strange purple night – dark yet glinting, like the moon on water – she could see well enough. She was a fast walker in ordinary circumstances, and this was not ordinary; she was seeking a safe place, beyond the realm of these thanes. They would come for her one day, but she would laugh. Shiel was a fortress. Let them besiege her.

Mary felt her way slowly through the castle. The soldiers slept so deeply it was like stepping over corpses. On the looming wall of the quadrangle the stairs made their sharp pattern, and Mary's eye traveled up to her balcony. No watchman paced!

At *her* castle, she would not be so careless; a patrol would always stalk her battlements. But this omission meant she could go up to her own room. There were two things she planned to take.

Folded in a small square of vellum, lying on a shelf in her little room, was a lock of her mother's hair. Next to it, her other treasure: the bracelet her father had carved from a whale tusk and given to Mother when they were young.

Malcolm, the older and more important prince, would have Mary's bed. It was too narrow to share, so the younger brother, Donalbain, would be on Aelgitha's trundle cot. How deeply would the princes sleep? Toast after toast had been drunk to them, and certainly they had declined no opportunity to lift a glass. Mary could probably slam the door and kick the furniture and they wouldn't know. But since Malcolm had only just gone to bed, Mary would pause to hear the slow, even breathing of his sleep before she went in.

After those strange howls, the night had fallen queerly silent.
Hundreds of men and horses, and not a breath of sound. She
stumbled over someone's leg, and the sleeper groaned and said,
"Murder."

. . . sleep in spite of thunder.
ACT IV, SCENE 1

FLEANCE SET HIS FATHER'S SWORD AND DAGGER SAFELY DOWN AND collapsed on the bed they would share. He did not take off his clothes. The night was chilly enough to sleep in them. He was sick with shame. How many stupid things could he do all in a row? He couldn't ride a horse, couldn't pull a sword, couldn't kill a man, couldn't tell the truth, couldn't turn down a reward falsely given, and couldn't even say a kind word to a desperate girl but had to laugh at Lady Mary and make things worse.

And then to charge into a barn and find that he'd tried to knife an owl! And Prince Malcolm had seen and had to save that poor woman, Ildred.

At some point in the night he woke to find that his father had lain down beside him. Banquo's arm was heavy on Fleance's back. Nothing said love as much as the weight of affection. Fleance slept.

In their stalls, the horses stamped and kicked, lips curled back and great teeth bloodred in the gloaming. Owls cried, and ravens grew hoarse. A chimney blew down.

Fleance knew these things though he was not there, and in his dreams the earth bubbled like water.

Stars, hide your fires!
Let not light see my black and deep desires.
ACT I, SCENE 4

EYTON FOUND SWIN SLEEPING ON THE FLOOR BY THE KITCHEN FIRE. Ildred was huddled up against Dirle. But Lady Mary was not there.

The coals on the hearth should have gone out long ago or been banked under a blanket of ash, and yet they throbbed with a strange, sharp-edged fire. He lit a wall torch from the flames and held it high, inspecting pantry, storeroom, scullery, buttery, and even the cold room over the spring. He should never have left Lady Mary alone at the barn. He had expected Lady Macbeth to assign a watch over a girl who could not protect herself. But Inverness was as loose as a sack untied, its contents spilling out.

Where would Lady Mary go to stay safe and warm?

The chapel was a possibility. She was constantly offering prayer. There were those who had heard her pray for that traitor Macdonwald! He hoped this hadn't been reported to King Duncan or to Macbeth. Seyton threaded his way among the sleepers in the courtyard. How could there be so many? Had they multiplied in the night, like sheep in spring?

The chapel was empty.

He was surprised. It was clean, warm, and dry. Why hadn't Lady Macbeth assigned sleepers here? Seyton was exhausted. He could think of nowhere else to look for Lady Mary, so he might as well rest here himself. For sleep, he wanted dark, so he stuck his torch in a wall bracket outside the chapel, rolled up his cloak for pillow and blanket both, and tucked himself against a wall.

Sleep did not come.

In the dark he began to see things.

A dagger hung by itself in the empty air. Unsupported. Untouched.

Seyton's mouth went dry.

He felt for a weapon but had none. Was that his own dagger hanging there? Had he had so much to drink it was giving him visions?

Somebody breathed.

Seyton had checked every inch of this chapel in case Lady Mary had crept under the altar or behind a pillar. He was alone in here. And whatever else God and His saints could do, they couldn't breathe. Now Seyton couldn't breathe, either. Before his frozen eyes walked Macbeth, staring where Seyton had stared. "Is this a dagger before me?" Macbeth whispered.

Yes, thought Seyton.

"Thou firm-set earth," breathed Macbeth. "Hear not my steps."

But Macbeth owned this castle. His steps ought to ring out, so his people could run to attend him.

The chapel's single bell moved. It did not ring so much as shiver. Its half-music half-spoke, and Seyton half-shuddered.

Macbeth laughed harshly. "Hear it not, Duncan. It is a knell."

A knell was not just any bell ringing. It summoned mourners to a funeral. And when a bell rang without a man pulling its rope, the bell was telling of death to come. *Whose death?* thought Seyton. *Is it mine?*

The dagger quivered.

Macbeth seized it. He ran his thumb down the blade of the knife he had plucked from the air, and the bell rang one more time. "It summons you to heaven, Duncan," whispered Macbeth. "Or hell."

O horror, horror, horror! Tongue nor heart
Cannot conceive . . .
ACT II, SCENE 3

WHEN SEYTON HAD LEFT THE KITCHEN, SWIN STOOD UP. Dirle whimpered but did not bark. Swin followed Seyton, running her fingers along the stone walls to guide herself.

She checked the Great Hall first, but two soldiers lying cross-wise filled the doorway. She couldn't step over them, so Seyton hadn't, either. She went into the forecourt. It took a while for her eyes to get accustomed to the gloom. There, foot on the stairs, going up to her own bedroom as if this were any ordinary night of her life, was Lady Mary.

Did the girl not grasp how much trouble she was in already?

Now she wanted to make things worse, elbowing into a room given to royalty? Swin marched over. If she tripped on these kerns, so be it.

"Lady Mary! You come with me!"

Lady Mary looked at her with shock, and then shook her head.

Ildred was right about this girl! Little Mistress Laziness expecting to enjoy her soft mattress no matter what! Swin latched on to the girl's arm. Lady Mary's bones were as thin as a fox's. Only the well-born could be that frail; a peasant with so little meat would have died by now, unable to do the labor.

Tears ran down Lady Mary's face.

Swin wanted to bat her into the middle of next week but hung on to her temper. "It's just for tonight, Lady Mary. King Duncan's to leave in the morning, his men said so, and it's all but morning now. You'll be back in your own room tomorrow."

"Swin —"

"Not every soldier is tired, you know. Some of them have enough left to take a maiden. You sleep in the kitchen beside me." Swin marched her back, thinking, They better not give her to me as a scullery maid. Think she'd wring the necks of poultry? Chop the livers of sheep? Scour crusted food out of a cook pot?

Swin was all too aware of the men she had wakened when she stormed over to grab Lady Mary. The kitchen doors didn't bolt from the inside, so Swin kicked triangles of wood beneath each door to wedge them shut. The noise made the sleeping scullery maids stir.

"Listen to the night," muttered Jennet. "Full of evil, it is. No wedge of wood stops a Weird One."

"Go back to sleep," ordered Swin.

Jennet muttered. Ildred snored. Dirle's paws trembled. The wind found a corner of the castle and was hanging on to it, screaming to get inside. I will never sleep, thought Swin, and she slept. The long day shook her dreams like fever, and she woke to the final call to judgment.

It was a trumpet so loud, so forceful, Swin knew the end of the world had come. She was unready. God needed to give her more time.

Dirle howled. Ildred scrambled to her feet. Lady Mary sat up, flat and thin as parchment.

The trumpet sounded again. This time, the trumpeter missed a note, sounding all too earthly. Not reveille, not attack, not retreat, and not welcome. But not God, either.

Swin kicked the doors free and ran into the courtyard.

The sky was ugly, as if day had fought for its turn, but night had won.

The courtyard was packed with men swathed in capes, men lurching around, men rubbing their eyes.

Leaning over the upper balcony, bending into the courtyard as if to vomit, his back to the open door of Lord and Lady Macbeth's chambers, was Lord Lennox. "Awake!" he screamed, as if they hadn't heard the trumpet. "Get up! Get up! The King has been murdered."

CHAPTER 6

Make all our trumpets speak, give them all breath,
Those clamorous harbingers of blood and death.
ACT V, SCENE 6

DUNCAN — UPON WHOM GOD SMILED?

Murdered?

Ildred was stricken with fear and chills.

Duncan. For whom they had just won a war.

All around Ildred were soldiers who knew everything there was to know about sudden death. They were stunned. They tried to take up battle positions, scrambling to arm themselves, or stumbled in circles, trying to spot the enemy.

Somebody began jerking on the bell rope. It clanged over and over, not a pattern to signal alarm or attack: just crazed tolling.

Over them hung a sky white and slimy, like congealed fat.

On the balcony Lord Lennox stood alone. He was a tall, solid man, but without his fine clothing and bright cloak, he just looked old. He had spent his life as a warrior, and now he clung to the balcony rail like a lost child. No one joined him. No one wanted to be up there, where the sacred person of a king had been attacked.

Finally, another lord appeared in the courtyard, still dressing himself, and the men turned desperately to Macduff for leadership. Much younger than Lennox, Macduff was a stocky, friendly man who defeated argument with a roar of laughter and slew enemies with a roar of revenge. The men trusted him. When Macduff clambered up the stairs, they stared after him, sure that he would make everything all right. Macduff plunged into the rooms that had been assigned to the King.

The courtyard was silent, waiting, needing what Lord Lennox had not given them: good news.

But from Macduff came a howl of sorrow, thin and lonely, like a wolf on the hill.

Two great warriors had been unmanned by what they saw in that room?

Ildred fled to the kitchen, still heated by last night's coals, still filled with the rich smell of the feast. She took Dirle in her arms for comfort. The dog licked her face and hands. She held Dirle tight – whether to protect the dog or hoping the dog would protect her, Ildred did not know.

To die in war was normal, although kings were largely kept off the actual field of battle. But to be murdered – a king! – no.

Ildred did not believe it. Duncan would have been guarded through the night, with sentries at his door. And what about those two annoying menservants? They would have been between the King and the door through which his murderer must come.

King Duncan died in his sleep, Ildred told herself, and Lennox and Macduff have panicked.

Yet at dinner, King Duncan had been so strong and fine. Not young – a dozen years older than his cousin Macbeth – but not old, either. In his prime. How could he have died in his sleep? And Lennox and Macduff were not children to panic in the presence of death.

Ildred went back out the kitchen passage, her back pressed against the stones, heart pounding so hard even the stones knew it.

At last came Lord Macbeth, shoving and shouting questions. He didn't believe this any more than Ildred did. He took the stairs two at a time to reach his own balcony.

Ildred frowned. But where does my lord come from? He and my lady slept last night in the room over the chapel. I prepared it for them. He approaches from the other direction.

She shook herself. This was Macbeth's castle; it was proper for him to be in each and any corner of it. He had a thousand guests, if you counted those out in the fields, and a thousand things to do.

Macbeth pushed past Lennox and Macduff into his own chambers, and at that same moment, the two princes stumbled out of Mary's room. The princes blundered around on the balcony like oxen, slow and confused.

"What is it?" shouted Malcolm. There was nothing royal about him. Nothing of a future king in his bearing. He was just a young man who had drunk too much the night before, and he was frightened. Ildred wanted to run to him, and dress him, and help him behave as a prince should.

The bell stopped ringing. The trumpet was silent. Into the sudden quiet Macduff said, "My princes, your royal father is murdered."

Prince Donalbain put a hand to his mouth like a girl.

But Malcolm was made of finer stuff. "Who did it?" he demanded.

Now on the run came Lord Banquo and his boy, Fleance, and then all the lesser lords: Ross, Caithness, Menteith, and Angus. The thanes stormed the balcony. The people remained below, clamoring for information.

"Our king was stabbed," Lennox told them. "Many times. With great violence."

As one, the people crossed themselves, every mouth saying, *"No, God!"*

Ildred thought, It will not be God who did it. It will be man.

. . . I have seen
Hours dreadful and things strange . . .
ACT II, SCENE 4

H ERE'S THE PRIEST!" CAME THE SHOUT, AND THE CROWD MADE
room for Father Ninian to pass. He wasn't good on
stairs, and in the commotion he might fall. They
helped him up. If there was still time, if there was still hope, King
Duncan must have prayers to take him on his way or catch up
if he had already set out into the next world.

Swin folded her strong arms over her broad chest. She was
filled with contempt for all these lords, running around like a
flock of brainless hens. The princes puzzled her. Everybody else
was dashing into the bedroom to see what had happened. But
neither Malcolm nor Donalbain did.

It's your father! thought Swin. Go see!

Prince Malcolm did a strange and un-royal thing. He stepped
backward, closer to his brother. They stayed on their side of the
balcony, as if they were afraid. True royalty were never fearful;
they had God on their side. This was the next king? What a
shame.

Swin looked around for Lady Mary.

What had the girl been doing up so late last night? Why had
she been standing on that stair? Had she been going up – *or
coming down*? The girl herself was white bread soaked in white

milk: soggy, bland, and not big enough to break a fast with, let alone kill a king. But if she had money, she could have bribed the servants.

But she doesn't have money, thought Swin, and why would a servant of Duncan do what she said anyway? Swin pulled her hood over her head and slumped against a wall to hide her great strength. Let no one remember that Swin used knives every day to kill and that for Swin, the spilling of blood was nothing.

<hr />

. . . I burned in desire to question them further . . .
ACT I, SCENE 5

<hr />

MEN WHO HAD BEEN POWERFUL IN BATTLE WERE NOW LIMP as wet linen. Seyton shoved through the crowd and met no resistance. Up the stairs he went, past the knot of horrified thanes, and into the solar. It amazed him that not everybody wanted to see the body with their own eyes. How could you believe it unless you looked at it?

The solar was a pretty room. Seyton had been entertained there, when Lady Macbeth had her guests in an intimate setting. She liked to have a harpist and singing and talk. It was always filled with sweet scent, because the lady loved perfume and kept dried roses and cinnamon in bowls.

Last night, only the servants of King Duncan had been assigned here. Now Seyton gaped. They were still in bed and still asleep! How could they sleep through screams and trumpets and bells?

The stench of liquor filled the room; more smell than could possibly come from the men's breath. Wine had spilled all over their bedclothes. But not all the dark stains were wine. Next to the two sleepers – right on their pillows – were knives covered with blood and gore. These two had killed the King? Seyton would have said they had as much courage and ability as Fleance, which was none.

Macbeth loomed over the servants, clenching and unclenching his fists. Seyton could not begin to imagine his wrath. Fine victory, fine castle, fine feast – forever stained by the murder of a sacred king.

Seyton took a quick look into the bedroom. The King's white head flopped off the side of the bed. Blood had spattered the far walls and dripped to the floor and threaded the ceiling. What force had been used! Had Duncan fought back, or had the killer been so filled with fear and horror that he stabbed as if killing ten men?

"If I had been hired to kill someone," Seyton said to his lord Macbeth, "I wouldn't lie down in the next room, waiting to be found." Although to kill a man, a man would have to get himself very drunk. Perhaps the servants had just staggered backward and fallen over.

Seyton and Macbeth stood together staring at the murderers.

Macbeth's chest heaved with emotion. *"They killed Duncan. Our gracious good King Duncan! Under my roof!"*

The servants, thought Seyton, would never have thought of murdering their master. So someone had paid them or forced them. Not the princes. Handsome and spirited, yes. But clever? No. Not that Seyton could see anything clever about this murder.

Last night, Seyton would have said Malcolm was not particularly interested in being king. Delighted by his many new friendships, yes; enjoying the party, yes. But it was easier to laugh away the night when one was *not* the king. So if not the princes . . .

Well, there were methods to get answers from helpless men. They would soon know who had hired these two.

"My dear good Duncan," said Macbeth suddenly. "My beloved king!" His hands flashed out. He seized the bloody knives with which the King had been slaughtered, shouting, "I avenge thee!"

A dream Seyton had had last night, a dream of daggers hanging in the air, a dream of bells tolling and hands snatching, came back to him. In the mist of this dream, he saw his lord Macbeth stab each killer.

And stab them again.

And again.

. . . let us meet
And question this most bloody piece of work . . .
ACT II, SCENE 3

H OW STRANGE, THOUGHT MARY, THAT THE PRINCES WERE NOT going in to look at their father's body but were crowding back toward her own little room, as if it were a sanctuary. As if they needed sanctuary. As if they knew more than they were saying.

Father Ninian was being helped up the steep stairs to give absolution to the King, and Mary thought, He's too old for this. *God, take care of your servant Ninian.*

"It looks as if our dear King's own men did it," Lennox told the crowd. "His body servants are lying there in a drunken stupor. Their bloody knives are beside them on their pillows."

Prince Donalbain was stupefied. "Our servants killed him? I can't believe that!"

"Those two have been with us for years," protested Malcolm. "We trust them completely."

Just so had King Duncan trusted Mary's father. But it had turned out that Duncan was not good at knowing who could be trusted.

In a thousand hearts was this very question: Who could be trusted now?

Mary had not had time to think about the death of her own father, and now she must think about the even more dreadful death of the King. Who would murder Duncan? Not even Mary's father, for a righteous death on the battlefield was not murder.

Why would anyone kill a king?

To take his place, of course.

Who besides her own father yearned to be king?

The thanes lined up on the balcony, silent and shocked. They looked weary and scared, and eerily alike – as if the murder had taken the stuffing out of them and they were just sausage cases with hands.

Banquo especially seemed to have aged and weakened, but in

contrast, when the boy, Fleance, joined his father, *he* looked stronger and more a man.

Could *Fleance* have killed Duncan? The Weird Ones, after all, had proclaimed that Banquo's issue would be king. Fleance, like Mary, had been awake and wandering late into the night. But so had Seyton, who spoke kindly and gently – but moved on. Where had he been going? And then Prince Malcolm himself, and Ildred. And Swin.

When she caught my arm, thought Mary, did Swin know already what had happened in that chamber? Swin, who can put a knife through anything? Is it not *man* who killed Duncan, but *woman*?

Look like the innocent flower,
But be the serpent under it.
ACT I, SCENE 5

ILDRED WAS HORRIFIED TO SEE LADY MACBETH WEARING ONLY HER white nightdress. Ildred snatched a cloak from some soldier and rushed to cover her mistress before the eyes of men. But no man was looking. Even the beautiful lady of this castle was nothing but a woman, and the death of a king was the affair of men. How Ildred envied men who could decide what and how and when.

Lady Macbeth threaded through the crowd. Ildred, twice as wide, had trouble following.

The racket from the balcony was ridiculous. It seemed to Ildred that every single man who entered the death chamber had to scream when he saw the body of the King; stagger out to the balcony; lift his hands to the paste-white sky; and cry to merciful heaven for help.

If heaven had planned to help, or be merciful, Duncan wouldn't be dead. Ildred already had cause to know that mercy was scarce.

How Lady Macbeth must hate this! The castle of which she was so proud was defiled. But she would marshal her forces like a general, and there would be order where these foolish thanes were allowing chaos. Ildred had always thought her lady was filled from crown to toe with the strength usually given to men.

When Macduff saw Lady Macbeth he rushed down the stairs, holding up his hands to stop her progress. Macduff was one of their dearest friends, a constant visitor at Inverness, and he knew Lady Macbeth well enough to put his arms around her.

"I must go to the King!" cried Lady Macbeth. "I must help."

"No," said Macduff. "There is nothing for you to do, and this is nothing you should see."

Oh, to be married to a man so able to comfort, thought Ildred.

But not only was Macduff married, he had several tiny children about whom he loved to talk. His chicks, he called them.

Lady Macbeth clung to Macduff. Her hair was not arranged for the day, and the long, shiny, black tresses slid off her shoulders and against Macduff. Her white nightgown swirled around her tiny feet, and the blue military cloak Ildred had tossed over her shoulders fell off. She was exquisite. "But what has happened?" she cried. "I heard people say there's been a murder, but I don't believe it! Not in my home, not within my walls! All are safe and loved here. What has happened? Tell me!"

Macduff patted her shoulder helplessly.

I could have been sleeping in that solar, thought Ildred. I could have been in the very room when the murderer passed through. He could have killed me, too. Because I know the servants did not do it. They cared about chamber pots, not power.

The soldiers were whimpering. "What next, what next?"

Ildred was irked. Obviously, next they had to name a new king. It was dangerous for a people to be without a king. How wise of Duncan to have named Malcolm heir last night. Malcolm, so handsome and noble. So full of gentle reassurance.

And he likes dogs, thought Ildred. That's always a good sign.

Ildred had a swift dream in which Malcolm fell in love and begged Ildred to be his bride. Ildred could see it all – wedding, castle, and crown.

"Duncan was slaughtered in his sleep," said Macduff.

"Dear Duff," said Lady Macbeth shakily. "I pray you. Say it isn't so."

Who did it? Ildred wondered. Who wants that crown the most of all?

Cawdor, of course. And Mary his daughter was right here, inside these walls. Could Lady Mary have avenged her father's execution?

Up on the balcony, Lord Macbeth stumbled out of the murder room. He gripped Lennox's arms and then looked down into his courtyard, packed with people silent or mumbling, wild or weak, every man there with two faces, one for the world and one in his heart.

The chaos stopped in a quick unnatural way, like a waterfall pausing midair.

"I killed them," said Macbeth, as if discussing the weather.

No one breathed.

"Killed who?" said Lennox.

"His murderers." Macbeth's voice began to climb. "That they should just lie there, sleeping like babes, when they stabbed our king! I couldn't let them sleep on as if nothing had happened! They killed him so viciously that his blood is flung around the room like lace on the walls. So I killed them. *Murderers!*"

"What do you mean, you killed them?" yelled Macduff from the bottom of the stairs. "The servants? We haven't questioned them yet! They wouldn't murder for their own sakes! *You killed them before we found out who hired them?*"

"You're right," said Macbeth. "It was stupid. But I loved my king. I had no restraint."

"How will we know now?" screamed Macduff. His handsome face twisted with disgust and outrage. "How will we ever find out who ordered the murder of Duncan?"

Lady Macbeth fainted, falling in a heap of white gown and black hair at Macduff's feet.

S WIN WAS STRONG ENOUGH TO STUN AN OX, AND ILDRED, THOUGH not as strong, was just as big. Together they carried Lady Macbeth's slender body into the kitchen.

Mary had pinned Asleif's brooch to the inside of her gown. It could not be seen, but it was still evidence that she might have reason to wish King Duncan dead: His army had killed her betrothed, and his orders had hung her father. Fear washed over Mary like the sea in a storm.

From the balcony, Banquo took charge. "We must question everyone. This is a bloody piece of work, and we have no knowledge of it. Your killing of the servants does not help us," he said to Macbeth. "But as God is my witness, we will discover what vicious mind was behind this. Come! Everyone gather in the Great Hall."

"Everyone" never included girls. Mary stood still.

The castle became very busy: those who continued to scream or pray; those who began to investigate; and those who went on with life, tending horses or packing their bags. Only Mary was doing nothing, because she was nothing. A few soldiers stayed on the balcony where unwilling servants were already carrying buckets of water to sluice away the blood.

There was no way for Mary to go unseen into her bedroom.

She would have to leave behind her mother's lock of hair and her father's ivory. She had been given one more chance to start for Shiel. The entire staff and Ildred would be in the kitchen, gathered around Lady Macbeth. Every lord and page had gone into the Great Hall.

As for the rest of the castle, chaos had struck everywhere. The wide double gate actually hung open. There was neither sentry nor porter.

Fog had rolled in off the North Sea, and it was lucky Mary knew the roads, because she would have to travel by the feel underfoot, not by sight. Mary stepped through the gates, took two paces only, and heard men's voices all too near. She pressed herself against the outer castle wall, hoping a few rags of fog would shelter her from their sight.

The two princes walked out. What on earth were Malcolm and Donalbain doing here? Why were they not with Lord Banquo, asking questions and demanding answers? Or kneeling beside their father's body, weeping and praying?

"We have to make plans," said Malcolm. "They'll blame this on us."

"No, they won't," argued Donalbain. "We're his sons; we would never hurt our father! Malcolm, we have to go to this meeting."

"No. Someone in this castle committed that murder," said Malcolm.

"The servants did it, Malcolm. Lennox, Macbeth, and Macduff all said so."

"I *might* believe that our servants' hands held the dagger — although I don't. But who hired them, if that's how it was? Or who really stabbed our father, if *that's* how it was? Every man in that hall will be shedding tears, Donalbain, and who's to say which tears are real?"

"If only Macbeth hadn't killed them," said Donalbain. "We could have asked a hundred questions."

"The first question," said Prince Malcolm, "is why Macbeth killed our servants."

Donalbain was surprised. "To avenge our father."

"I doubt that. The nearer in blood to a king," said his older brother, "the more the death of that king matters. Who is nearest to our father in blood, after us? Our father's cousin is. Macbeth himself."

Like a blanket, Mary folded down on the cold, wet ground. The son of murdered King Duncan believed that Macbeth, *with his own hand*, had killed the King.

What if such a thing were true?

It couldn't be. Macbeth was a good man.

On the other hand, her father had been a good man. What made a man good? Did Mary still know? *Were* there any good men?

And if Malcolm was right? Poor Lady Macbeth! When she recovered from her faint, she would hear this rumor that the husband she loved, with whom she hoped to have sons of her own, was a murderer.

"Malcolm," said Donalbain. His voice was whiny. Mary had not noticed this before. "If we're not at the inquiry, they'll blame this murder on us."

"They'll blame us anyway."

"Then what shall we do?"

"Run."

"But where?" said Donalbain, horrified.

Indeed, thought Mary, that's the problem I found with running.

"I'll go to England, you to Ireland. It's safest to be apart. One of us ought to survive."

There was a padding sound, more like the paws of dogs than the boots of men. The sons of a king were sneaking down the hill.

Mary could not seem to rouse herself. The mud was cold and horrid, and yet she could not seem to stand. She was wasting time lying here. She, too, must run.

A patch of fog lifted, giving her a momentary glimpse of the princes, riding away. Where had they found horses? Just taken them, she supposed, from all those tethered in the field.

The sons of dead Duncan – stealing horses and running.

And what would happen when the thanes in the hall learned about this? They would indeed blame the sons for Duncan's murder. The army would comb the hills and crawl through glens.

If Mary ran, that army – angry, vengeful, and very familiar with the countryside – would find her in a minute. She was stuck at Inverness.

With a murderer.

CHAPTER 7

Yet do I fear thy nature.
ACT I, SCENE 5

I LDRED WAS ASTONISHED WHEN LADY MACBETH ALLOWED SWIN – A kitchen girl! – to put an arm around her and pat her back. "Here, my lady," said Swin, ladling out some of her excellent barley soup, rich with lamb bones and leftovers. "Nice hot soup. This will strengthen you."

Ildred had never imagined Lady Macbeth needing strength. In fact, Ildred would not have imagined Lady Macbeth fainting to start with. This was a woman who prided herself on handling anything with poise and assurance.

How rigidly Lady Macbeth was sitting; how shallow and nervous was her breath. Ildred softened. This wanting-est of women had so wanted a king in her very own castle, dining at the table she had set, drinking from her fine new goblets beneath the tapestry she had woven. How she had basked in the attention of all those thanes and the King himself. How she had flirted with the princes! With what pleasure she bustled around, making the sleeping arrangements, proving that she actually could put up hundreds of guests in this relatively small place.

Nobody would remember that.

They would remember only that, under her roof, a king was murdered.

The lady was holding her hands together. She did not take the cup Swin offered. "Ildred, did you see the King?" she asked.

How could Ildred have gone anywhere or seen anything? She had been standing next to Lady Macbeth – or holding her. "No," she said.

Swin kept glancing toward the chapel. Did she want to be out there with everybody else, chasing murderers? Ildred didn't. She had met a murderer once before and did not want to know another one.

Lady Macbeth opened one hand and looked down into it, as if reading her own palm. Ildred gasped. Lying in her hand was a diamond, its facets sparkling with inner fire. It was not set in a ring or pendant. Where had it come from? Ildred knew all Lady Macbeth's jewels. And if she had time to get jewelry this morning, why didn't she have time to get properly dressed?

Ildred looked closely at Lady Macbeth. Could she have pretended to faint? Hoped her husband would hurtle down the stairs to tend her in front of all those men?

It struck Ildred forcibly that this most attentive of husbands had not come to his wife's side. Had not sent anyone to the kitchen to check on her. Was it because he knew perfectly well that she was fine?

Lady Macbeth held the diamond up to the flames to increase its glitter. "As King Duncan left the hall last night, I stood on tiptoe and he bent down and kissed my cheek." Lady Macbeth caressed the cheek a king had kissed. "But Duncan forgot he'd brought a gift for me. While the thanes were putting him to bed, he remembered, and handed my gift to Banquo to pass on to me." She referred to Banquo as if he were of no more significance than Ildred.

While the thanes were putting the King to bed, thought Ildred. According to the sleeping arrangements Lady Macbeth made . . . the very strange sleeping arrangements.

Lady Macbeth forgot the diamond. "My bedroom must be ruined," she said fretfully. "All that blood everywhere."

"The maids will clean it up," said Ildred. "You won't see one spot of blood once they're done." But it won't be me cleaning it. And I'm not sleeping in that solar ever again, either.

"Besides," said Swin, also riveted by the diamond, "good Macbeth killed those as done it. Nothing else can happen now, my lady. Except somebody else has to be named king."

Ildred nodded. "Malcolm," she said, tasting his name, glad for the chance to use it. She touched the shoulder Malcolm had patted last night. Was it possible that somebody somewhere would love Ildred? Might it even be Malcolm?

"I'll never be able to tell Duncan how grateful I am," said Lady Macbeth, and this seemed to amuse her. The crooked triangle of her smile spread wider, until she almost laughed, and then her smile came apart, and her face was distorted by fear. Something was on her nightgown. She mumbled at it, and brushed at it, but the clean white cloth was bare of anything except lace. Lady Macbeth smacked it, as if killing wasps, and then leaped up, trying to get away from her own clothes. The diamond was flung across the room, hitting the floor and skittering into the shadows. "There's blood on me!" she shrieked.

"No, there isn't," said Ildred.

Swin – they said as how Swin knew things others didn't – Swin backed away from Lady Macbeth. She became a kitchen girl again, keeping pots and tables between herself and the lady.

Ildred caught the lady's wrist. "You weren't even there," she said firmly. *Or were you?* "There is no blood on you. Hush now. Sit back down." To pat her lady's temple and throat, Ildred dipped a clean rag into the basin of hot water that was always sitting at the edge of the coals.

Lady Macbeth began to wash her hands. She scrubbed each finger one by one.

Swin stirred the great kettle of barley broth. Her lips moved. Is she praying for Lady Macbeth's health? wondered Ildred. Or is Swin one of the Weird Ones?

No. If Swin had powers, she'd use them to get a better place to sleep than a kitchen floor.

Lady Macbeth dropped the rag in the basin and spoke in her usual voice. "Ildred, find my diamond."

Ildred crept over the floor.

The diamond was not there.

Since the kitchen floor was packed dirt, there were no cracks between stones into which a diamond could fall. Ildred had seen it roll. She knew where it had to be. Yet even when she removed everything from that end of the room, still the diamond was not there.

"'Cause he was murdered," said Swin. "The dead-lights took it."

Ildred was afraid to look around, lest she should see the glow of a lost soul.

God save the King!
ACT I, SCENE 2

F LEANCE HAD JUST STOOD ON A BATTLEFIELD. HE HAD JUST SEEN Brude turned into a corpse in an instant. Brude had died by slashes because that was how death came in war – from a sharp edge. But the King's body was different. Slashed, yes, but not honorably. This was a death foully done in the dark against an unarmed man in his sleep.

The thick white hair was spattered with blood, the finely woven night tunic torn and stained. The arms hung over the sides of the bed, limp, as if they had never had the strength to wield a sword.

With such grief did Duncan's men leave their meeting in the hall. How soberly they walked up those stone stairs, two by two. How tenderly they carried him down for the last time. With tears, they laid Duncan to rest in the chapel.

Father Ninian went down on his knees beside the body and prayed in Latin. The thanes did not want to pray. They wanted to fight.

When Lady Mary knelt, the officers gave her a hard look, not wanting the traitor's daughter there. Nobody interfered. They were unwilling to prevent a girl from prayer.

Probably, thought Fleance, they think she's meek and mild, like a saint.

Fleance knew better.

I'm the one who's meek and mild, he thought, despising himself.

When Father Ninian had completed the first round of prayers, Banquo had had enough. He summoned the men back to the Great Hall. Fleance stood at his father's side. "It is understandable," said Banquo, "that great Macbeth lost his temper in rage and revenge. But no one must follow his example."

Macbeth shot Banquo an unreadable look, folded his arms over his chest, and silently surveyed the thanes.

Banquo's warning meant nothing to the younger officers. They did not want a sermon on how to behave. "Before we worry about the murderer," they yelled, "let's acclaim Prince Malcolm king!"

"Malcolm!" came the shouts. "Let Malcolm decide how to avenge his father's murder!"

But Malcolm could not be found.

Neither was there any trace of Donalbain.

They searched over and over, peering in the same places, calling the same names.

Once more it was Lord Lennox giving the news. "The princes have fled!" he said, his voice hoarse with disbelief and horror. "They took two horses tethered by the gate and *ran*."

The shock of Duncan's murder was not as deep as the shock of finding out who the killers were: Duncan's sons.

Fleance was stunned. Why would they run? That did not add up. If Malcolm had planned this murder, and was guilty of it, he'd stay to reap the reward. To be crowned king himself. But both brothers cut and ran? They who had the finest of horses and the best of saddles had stolen old nags?

Somebody collected Father Ninian, whose trembling old hands made the sign of the cross. Hundreds made the sign with him, but Fleance did not feel blessed. He felt under the banner of evil.

I know nothing about my fellow man, thought Fleance. How right King Duncan was. He said you could not know a man's thoughts by his face. I thought Malcolm was so princely. He was kind to that fat woman I almost stabbed and kind to me when I was an idiot. Did he really walk away from us, climb the stairs, and say to his two loyal servants – Now is a good time. Go in there and murder my father?

Fleance would never have believed it. Yet they had run.

He listened to the brief suggestion from one lord that Duncan's cousin Macbeth should be named king. Listened to a second lord agree. Saw a few men nod. Acclamation meant saying yes by shouting and yelling. This was something else: frightened acceptance.

Lord Macbeth was very sober. He received the charge, and he agreed.

The men stood and saluted.

It seemed to Fleance that Macbeth waited for cries of joy.

There were none.

⌇

Go pronounce his present death
And with his former title greet Macbeth.
ACT I, SCENE 2

⌇

ARY STEPPED INTO THE PRAYERS, LEANING ON THE LATIN. Even with the world in collapse, she could find the peace of God which passeth all understanding. And the sweet saints, who always stayed so close, put their arms around her.

Father Ninian chanted so beautifully. Perhaps it was his great age. He had used these prayers so long he could render every syllable so sweetly.

A soldier in arms strode into the chapel, roughly interrupting them. "Father!"

The priest was so deep in his prayers he had to be shaken by the shoulder, and Mary thought it shook his heart as well.

"The princes have run," said the soldier. "They killed the king, their own father. Come. Now."

Father shuffled out, looking back with longing for his altar and his unfinished prayers.

"Amen," Mary said for him.

The chapel door hung open. Outside, the sky had darkened as if it were night. Rain pelted the castle, pouring off the roof in torrents and puddling in the courtyard. If the heavens ever spoke, they were speaking now, because this was fugitive weather. Bad for comfort, good for safety. Few soldiers would go out in this downpour to hunt for missing men. The princes could put many miles between themselves and their pursuers.

There was not enough roof for shelter. Most people had to stand in the open like cattle and get drenched. "But who will be king?" they said, voices filled with fear.

Lennox seemed to hesitate. He cleared his throat. Then he spoke carefully, as if removing himself from the decision. "The men have acclaimed Macbeth. Father Ninian has placed his hand upon the hand of Macbeth and prayed for him as God's representative on earth. Macbeth is king."

Mary stared out the still open gate, where the countryside was already flooding in low places.

Hail Macbeth, who shall be king hereafter.

So it was not chance, after all, that had crowned Macbeth.

It was murder.

What, can the devil speak true?
ACT I, SCENE 3

L ORD ROSS CAME TO THE KITCHEN. ILDRED WAS STILL ON THE FLOOR, searching for the gem. She knew Lord Ross would not see her. A servant was just another tool. She could be a pot or a pan for all Lord Ross would notice. How big and brawny he was. How fortunate his pretty wife, filling their castle with children. While I, Ildred thought, crawl on my knees in the dirt.

He bowed, looking strangely awkward. Then he kissed Lady Macbeth's hand. "Your husband," he said, as if he could not get his mind around this, as if the words might be in some foreign tongue, "is king."

Lady Macbeth forgot the diamond. She forgot Ildred crawling on the floor. She forgot Lord Ross himself. "*King*," she repeated. She held out her arms to embrace the word. A queer smile of triumph engulfed her face. "*My husband.* My fine and brave husband." She hugged herself. "Not too full of the milk of human kindness after all. Ildred, go to my room. I must be well dressed. There will be ceremonies. I will have to welcome many new guests. Get my ruby-red gown and the gold circlet for my hair. I'll want my gold chains and my best slippers, the ones with the flowers."

The milk of human kindness?

Ildred thought of milk, and mothers who gave milk to baby

animals or infant children, and she thought of the death of babies, and then she was defeated. She could not obey. She could not go into a room where a king had died at a murderer's hand.

Ildred tottered away. The courtyard was filled with people as unsteady and unready as Ildred was. Across the way stood Lady Mary, apparently unaware that rain was soaking her. Ildred walked over. "Lady Macbeth instructs you to get her clothing. She isn't dressed yet, and people will be coming."

Mary looked as stunned as if she had been hit between the eyes with a mallet, the way Swin would hit an ox before she slit its throat. It didn't seem to occur to Mary that she could refuse. Ildred gave her a list of necessities, and the girl nodded dimly and walked toward the stairs as if wading through water.

After his soldiers had brought down their king's body, no one had stayed on that balcony. The whole floor had been abandoned. Mary would have to walk alone into a room where a murder had happened, step over the blood, and fumble through a trunk while the unquiet spirit of Duncan hovered.

Serves you right for not sharing your bedroom, thought Ildred. She looked around for somebody who knew something and found Fleance. "I thought they would acclaim Malcolm," she said to him. "King Duncan named Malcolm his heir."

"Malcolm's the killer," said Fleance dully.

"Nonsense."

"The princes ran. They've taken to the hills."

"That doesn't mean they murdered their own father," whispered Ildred.

"What does it mean, then?" asked Fleance.

But Ildred had no answer.

The thanes came slowly out of the hall and into the rain. They stared up at the heavens, stared down at mud and through the main gates. Malcolm and Donalbain had murdered their own father? In one hour, Scotland had lost her beloved king *and* his two dear sons?

The rain seized Ildred's tears and rushed them off her face. It soaked through her clothing and into her heart.

Look on it again I dare not.
ACT II, SCENE 2

MARY MADE IT UP THE STAIRS. SHE LOOKED ALL AROUND THE balconies. No one was here. She checked the doors. No one stood guard. She glanced back down into the courtyard. No one was looking up. Not simply by herself but not noticed by another human being, Mary of Shiel had to walk into a murder room. A thousand miles across a haunted moor would have been easier.

She edged into the solar. There, on the great soft mattress that served as couch by day, where ladies lounged and sang and chattered, were two dead men. Their eyes were open.

Mary sidled past, her back against the wall. The room stank of wine. How inexplicable that after conspiring to murder, they would drink themselves into a stupor and take a nap. Why weren't they the ones racing around the Highlands trying to escape?

From the bedchamber itself came a scuffling noise. Mary's knees gave way for the second time. Duncan's ghost? Scrabbling to find his body? Mary was crawling now and whimpering. On the other side of the door something else whimpered – and then whined – and Mary said, "Dirle? Are you trapped in there?"

She pushed open the bedroom door, and her nose met the cold, happy nose of a small dog. Dirle skittered and yapped and licked. Then, because he was a dog, he became deeply interested in the rich bloody scents of wall, floor, and bed.

Mary picked him up for company and forced herself into the murder chamber.

The mattress was gone, but nothing had been scrubbed. The servants had carried in buckets of water, then just set them down and fled. A little puddle of Duncan's lifeblood lay between her and the chests in which Lady Macbeth's clothing lay.

Clinging to Dirle, Mary took a giant step over the puddle. She opened the trunk where the ruby-red gown lay carefully folded. If only life could be arranged so neatly.

She needed to set Dirle down in order to carry everything Lady Macbeth required. A few minutes passed before Mary could part with his warm, comforting little body. Then she took the gown and slippers and was opening the jewelry box when Seyton walked into the room, quietly closing the heavy door behind him.

Whatever he had been expecting, it wasn't Mary. He gasped.

Dirle growled, snapping at Seyton and biting at his boots. "Dirle!" she said, trying to corral the dog. "I'm sorry, sir. He's usually friendly."

"I'm usually friendly, too," said Seyton, smiling. He had such a fine smile. Laugh lines ran deep into his cheeks.

Mary had to get out of this horrible room. She couldn't paw through the jewelry until she found the right piece. She took the whole box.

"I'm worried about you, Lady Mary," said Seyton. "When Lord Macbeth has had time to get used to being King, I'll put in a good word for you. I don't believe, the way everybody else does, that you knew ahead of time what your father was doing."

Everybody believed that? Did Lady Macbeth? How would Mary ever establish that she, too, could be loyal? That she *was* loyal! Had *always* been loyal!

She managed to get Dirle under her arm. Dogs were supposed to be the most loyal of all, but Dirle was loyal mainly to dinner. Holding Lady Macbeth's gown so it did not drag on the floor, and keeping Seyton between her and the dead men, Mary stumbled to the balcony. When she could breathe again, she thought, *If Macbeth is King, Lady Macbeth is Queen.*

Queen Macbeth.

Ah, good father,
Thou seest the heavens . . .
ACT II, SCENE 4

ATHER NINIAN HAD GOTTEN COMPLETELY WET. HE WAS SO OLD AND
frail. Ildred took one of the old altar cloths that had not
been used to wrap the corpse of the King and toweled her
priest dry. He protested but gave in because he was trembling
from the chill.

"There," she said, having started with his head and hair and
finishing up with his toes. It had put her in a strangely good
mood to care for the priest. On her knees she smiled up at him.
"Now you can finish the prayers for King Duncan."

"First, my daughter, let us pray for you."

Her good mood evaporated. "I hate being prayed for," she
snapped.

Father Ninian paid no attention. He rested his thin blue-veined
fingers on Ildred's forehead. "Dear Lord, have mercy on your
daughter Ildred. What is more terrible for a mother than to lose
a babe? What is more terrible for a girl than to be alone? What is
more terrible for a woman than to have no hope? Bring your
daughter Ildred love and renew her hope."

Ildred's throat closed. "What do you know?" she whispered.

"Not enough, my daughter. If I had known enough, I would
have helped."

"I thought he would find the baby a home!" Ildred cried. "He said he knew a family to love her, but he took her outside and abandoned her to the weather. Father, is it true? Did they – well, hurt the baby in some way?"

"She was perfect, Ildred. If she had lived, what a fine child she would have been."

"I sinned."

"Yes. And you have truly repented. And God forgives."

"I don't want forgiveness. I want my baby." She rested her face on his knobby old knee and wept.

Send out more horses, skirr the country round . . .
ACT V, SCENE 3

IN SPITE OF ORDERS FROM MACBETH, NOBODY WAS EAGER TO CHASE THE princes.

Weather was the soldiers' excuse. Every burn would flood, and every bog would quake; every boot fill with water, and every horse slide in the mud.

But it wasn't really the rain, Swin thought. The sons of Duncan had been loved. No one wanted to find them.

Macbeth's troops beat the bushes of the glens and searched the huts of the wilderness. As the days passed, they also herded the people down to Inverness. Huge would be the crowd that saw Macbeth acclaimed king.

But the crowd was unwilling. Dark and forced were their cheers.

They had loved Duncan. They did not want to believe that his two fine sons had killed him. Against all evidence, they would rather have had Malcolm.

Swin wondered if Lord and Lady Macbeth knew this. Lady Macbeth was delirious with excitement and pride. Where Swin saw sad soldiers, Lady Macbeth saw her husband honored. Where Swin saw mourners, Lady Macbeth saw troops of friends.

Swin's grandfather would be hungry. Yet here she was again, feeding a huge crowd. Easy enough to stash away food for him, but Swin could not leave her responsibilities and go to him. Nor would it be safe. As soon as the rain ceased, the hills were going to fill with soldiers, poking in every hut and cottage. Macbeth wanted to hang Donalbain and Malcolm – and who knew, if a king was in a hanging mood? Might he take out his wrath on a kitchen maid caught stealing his food?

. . . float upon a wild and violent sea . . .
ACT IV, SCENE 2

MARY HAD GIVEN HER FIRST CURTSY TO THE NEW QUEEN. Fastened the clasp on a gown that now dressed a queen. The whole time Mary was tying her sash, the Queen was walking forward. Mary had to crawl along, tugging the hems down so the fabric would fall evenly. "My husband," Lady Macbeth kept whispering. "The King."

She's practicing for her procession, thought Mary. For when they have the real ceremony at Scone. Just as my father practiced for his execution.

The Queen marched out of the room, and Mary let go of the hem. She had been sleeping in the kitchen, but now courage returned. Mary followed the Queen but did not join her. She moved slowly, silently, into her own tiny chamber. Untouched and safe on their little shelf were her two treasures. She slipped them into a silk bag where she was now keeping the brooch of Asleif safe and tied the bag at her waist under her full skirt. Then she made two decisions.

First, she would not run. She wanted to be full of virtue. Loyalty was the greatest virtue. If you ran, you were not loyal.

Second, she would not entertain doubts about her new king. She wanted the Macbeths to trust her, and therefore she had to trust them. Macbeth said that Prince Malcolm and Prince Donalbain had killed their father, so they had. That day on the moor Mary had promised herself to follow the strong and good example of Lady Macbeth. Now she must do it.

Yet when Mary looked around her cozy little room, she could not imagine Malcolm and Donalbain lying here, planning their father's murder. And when she had overheard them speak to each other, just before they ran, they had not sounded guilty but loyal.

Loyalty had layers. If Mary stayed loyal to her father, she was disloyal to Duncan. If she stayed loyal to Macbeth, she was disloyal to Duncan's sons.

My father put me here, she told herself. I stay loyal to him by believing that he made wise choices for me. Macbeth is now king. I stay loyal to him by believing – what?

What did she believe?

Mary tripped on something. She looked down. Malcolm and Donalbain had fled without their belongings. Mary knelt and poked through the pile. She was now the owner of two sets of men's clothing, a pair of good boots, a perky little woolen cap, a leather knapsack well made, and two fine sharp dirks.

She packed the knapsack. At the bottom went one of her own gowns, an old heavy wool in a dark color, and on top of that, the little silk bag with her three treasures. Then she added the smaller trousers, cap, and tunic – probably Donalbain's, since he was the younger – and tucked in one dirk, safely pointing down. She tied the knapsack shut and hung it on the wall peg under her cloak.

The second dirk she fastened to her waist. Just in case.

MACBETH IN THIS GREAT EMERGENCY GAVE ORDERS. THE soldiers – eager to be told what to do – obeyed. The servants – afraid of change – obeyed. Hundreds hurried off, as if the speed of their obedience would ward off any more dreadful events.

But the days passed, and evil kept its grip. The horses would not calm down. The owls and ravens would not go silent. The rain stopped, but the skies moved too early to sunset, spreading bloody clouds over Scotland, like piles of the dead on the shore.

CHAPTER 8

Give me the daggers.
ACT II, SCENE 2

THE CROWNING WAS SWIFT, AND THERE WAS LITTLE CEREMONY.

"King!" shouted the people, and Macbeth lifted his hand to acknowledge them. With a sweep of his arm, he gestured to his beautiful wife, and the people were pleased. A queen was good and fair, and the sight of her softened thoughts of murder and killers. Just as Macbeth — burly and imperious — made such a fine king, so did Lady Macbeth — beautiful and elegant — make a fine queen.

Every thane, landholder, and man of rank approached Macbeth. "Sire, I become your man."

An oath as binding as marriage, Seyton thought, and he looked to see if little Lady Mary was watching. She was no eagle like Lady Macbeth — wide of wing and sharp of talon. Mary was lovely in a passive way, as women should be, as his mother had been. Born for obedience and service.

Seyton yearned for Mary, so frail and shy, almost as much as he yearned for her title and lands.

The Macbeths seemed to have forgotten Lady Mary, as indeed they seemed to have forgotten the title and land of Cawdor. Seyton would have felt his life worthwhile if he had been given Cawdor by a king. Perhaps it happened so fast that they had no time to realize that they owned and were Cawdor until they also owned and were Scotland. Now Cawdor would just be one castle among many, one title among a dozen.

But Lady Mary was not just one girl among many.

What did Seyton have to offer her — or to offer *for* her? Nothing.

What could he be that nobody else could be? Nothing.

Could he instead *do* something nobody else could do?

What might that be?

It was Banquo's turn to kneel before Macbeth. Only days ago the two men had been equal commanders in battle. Now Banquo touched his forehead to his knee and swore his oath. His pathetic son, Fleance, did the same. Poor Banquo, to have that weakling for a son. Seyton had set up Fleance as the destroyer of that soldier on the sand because you never knew when you might want a noble in your pocket. But Fleance wasn't worth having. And now it was too late for Seyton to take his rightful credit for the kill; that would only enrage Banquo.

Lord Lennox and Lord Macduff took their oaths. Ross and Menteith. Caithness and Angus. Macbeth took joy in every pledge. How he reveled in being king!

Seyton thought of that terrible hour in which he had witnessed Macbeth killing those servants, the extent of his rage and the violence of his attack. Perhaps, thought Seyton, there *was* one thing he could do that no one else would...he, too, could remove men who stood in Macbeth's way.

Seyton's turn came at last. He said the same pledge, but few paid attention, because the important men had finished. This was an advantage, because Seyton's pledge was longer than anybody else's. "Do any names blister your tongue, my king?" he said softly. "Tell me. I will remove them."

Your face, my Thane, is as a book where men
May read strange matters.
ACT I, SCENE 5

AND THEN THE CEREMONIES WERE OVER, AND MACBETH WAS riding to Scone, to be crowned the way a king must be crowned, in the right place at the right time with the right words. Three separate events, thought Ildred, in which Macbeth was officially named king. Three was a sacred number, but were all kings called three times? Or did Macbeth want to make very sure he really had the throne?

Ildred hurried upstairs to gather traveling clothes for Lady

Macbeth. The journey to Scone would be swift and hard. Ildred could not bear the thought of sitting on a horse herself or enduring the rattle and jarring of a cart. Since Lady Macbeth would need a companion, Ildred was presenting Lady Mary as the ideal company: a fine rider and obedient to the wishes of her queen. And, Ildred thought, too stupid to add one fact to the next and reach the terrible conclusion so many others had come to.

The staff had been forced to clean the solar and the bedchamber. Blood would not out. They slapped paint on some of the stains. The mattresses were dragged away to be burned. A new linen bag was sewn to hold fresh feathers for a new bed for the new king and queen.

Ildred considered what the lady needed. The weather looked to stay bad. Ildred would send the sheepskin cloak, although it was neither pretty nor queenly. But at the height of those mountain passes, in freezing rain, Lady Macbeth would be glad to wrap herself in thick fleece.

Ildred tiptoed into the solar, the first time she had entered since the murders. The couches had been repositioned. Tapestries taken from elsewhere in the castle were now hanging over the stained walls. The bodies of the two servant killers had been tossed into a ditch where not so many weeks ago a newborn babe had been left. It was a wicked world. Ildred wanted to be one of the good ones, but she wasn't; her heart and mind were full of sin. She wiped her eyes on her sleeve, and from inside the chamber where one king had been murdered she heard the voice of another king.

"I still hear that knocking," said Macbeth.

"Every noise appalls you now," said Lady Macbeth. "But it's over and all is well. A little water cleaned it up. Now smooth your thoughts and that will smooth your face."

Ildred waited patiently outside the door. She did not know where this patience came from. It was not usually one of her virtues, if she even had any virtues. Only Father Ninian had faith in her.

"When Father Ninian said God bless you, I could not say 'Amen,'" said Macbeth.

"Don't think deeply about it. What's done is done."

"You can do that, my chuck?" The new king sounded both sad and amazed. "You can let your thoughts die just as he died?"

Ildred was surprised and touched. Macbeth sounded as sad about Duncan as every other subject of that good king. It was her opinion that Lord Macbeth himself must have given the order to kill Duncan, yet here he was, on his way to Scone for his coronation, mournful and heartsick.

But Ildred was too sick at heart herself to worry about other hearts.

"Things without remedy should be ignored," said the new queen briskly.

My whole life is without remedy, thought Ildred. How can I ignore my life?

Ildred withdrew. She did not actually care whether the new queen had the right clothing for this trip on which Ildred was not going.

Will you to Scone?
No, cousin, I'll to Fife.
ACT II, SCENE 4

L ADY MACBETH WANTED TO GO TO SCONE, EVEN BEGGED TO GO, BUT the King refused. Mary had never seen Macbeth deny his wife anything. It would slow him down, he explained. Ladies could not ride fast or astride, and the King had no time for carriages or a gentle pace.

Macbeth seemed as glad to ride away from his queen as he was to ride toward his crown. He set out with flourishes of trumpets in a party of fine horses and eager young men. The older men had surrendered their places, for they had wives and children and crops to see to.

Or so they said.

There was relief on their faces when Macbeth disappeared over the hills. But Mary had no time to wonder why. The new queen gave her first decree: "We will not stay at Inverness. We cannot abide where two depraved princes killed their own dear father. We will move our court to the royal palace at Forres."

Mary was glad for her. Lady Macbeth would have the magnificent Great Hall she dreamed of and gardens full of flowers instead of cabbages. There would be a musicians' gallery and quarters for servants and barracks for soldiers. In that royal chamber would be chests filled with furs: ermine and martin and miniver. No doubt robes of purple and scarlet were piled high, and the vessels were made of silver and gold.

Or perhaps not. Wars were costly, and Duncan might have spent it all. And Duncan's wife having died so long ago, perhaps everything had fallen to mold and rust.

Wagons and oxcarts pulled into the courtyard to be filled. Kegs of ale and beer, sides of beef and mutton, great round cheeses and drooping sacks of flour and barley were loaded. Barrels and boxes, casks and jars, bags and chests; everything in the pantry and larder and buttery. Everything in the storerooms and out-buildings, attics and cellars.

She's never coming back, thought Mary. They will abandon Inverness and its stains of blood.

The road to Forres arched north and east along the rough shore, too far to travel in one day. The castle most convenient for an overnight was Cawdor. What would it be like to spend a night in her own home while the Queen and her court poked through the blessed space of Mary's childhood?

The Queen's ladies-in-waiting began arriving. The wife of Lord Ross came, two young sisters of Lord Caithness, and a cousin of Lord Menteith. How excited they were. No more elderly old kings surrounded by warriors. Now they had a handsome king and a beautiful young queen. They could dress well again, and entertain, and have fine jewels and grand parties.

Lady Ross was the most fun. To accept the honor of serving the new queen she left her two children at their castle in the far north. She was plump and cheerful and seemed to feel no gloom. When she tuned her little harp, she didn't sing sad ballads where everybody suffered and died and lost their true love. She struck up silly rollicking verses, where treasure from shipwrecks washed up on the sand and handsome pirates seized maidens who were happy to be bound and tied.

After peeking once at the murder scene, the ladies weren't eager to return to the solar. The Queen arranged room for herself and her ladies by curtaining portions of the Great Hall.

Lords Lennox and Ross went to Scone with the King.

Lord Macduff went home to Fife, to his favorite castle Falkland to see his wife and chicks. Mary loved how he called his children "chicks." He said it so affectionately, perfectly willing to be thought soft.

I want to be a wife with chicks, she thought. Oh, Asleif. You and Father did not do well by me.

Macduff had any number of castles in Fife, and it was on his shores that Mary's father had lost his battle. Why there? Why not on the same battleground where Asleif had died? Mary would never know. But it didn't matter. The world had lost interest in Cawdor.

Of the highest ranking officers, only Banquo was still at Inverness. Banquo, who had marshaled an army, now marshaled a court on the move. He supervised stewards and servants, carts and wagons. Always in a good humor, always with a bow to the new queen. How the Queen loved those bows. She treasured them as Mary treasured the lock of her mother's hair. It was touching that a queen could find it so joyful just *being* a queen.

The Queen hardly noticed Mary but gave Ildred twice as much work as one woman could handle. Mary took over the packing and sorting that Ildred hated, although sometimes Mary thought that what Ildred hated was being near those lovely ladies-in-waiting, because Ildred would never be one of them.

On the final day, all beds but the Queen's were dismantled, the frames unlocked, the leather laces rolled up, and the mattresses wrapped in sheets. Mary supervised the packing of them. She secured the leather tarpaulins herself to be sure the bedding would stay dry. She was carrying the last pile of folded linen when she tripped over Fleance. It was no surprise, since he was nothing but legs and arms sticking out where people had to walk.

"Sweet welcome, Lady Mary," he said eagerly.

It was an ordinary greeting, but theirs was not an ordinary relationship – he had killed Asleif. Mary steered around him, thinking, If only Swin had put a charm on Fleance! I'd still have Asleif, and this wretched little twig would be broken in half.

Fleance walked alongside her, as if they were friends. Mary was disgusted. Fleance assumed that since he and Mary were the same age and the same size, they would have the same thoughts.

"I was thinking," said Fleance, "that the King on his way to Scone must be following the very same route the princes took when *they* were running."

Macbeth would follow rivers, the Spey and the Garry and the Tay. Mary loved those rivers because they led to Shiel. Macbeth would not be so very far from Glamis, either, his father's castle, nor from Fife, where Macduff was even now hugging his chicks.

"Because the princes couldn't have gone north," said Fleance. "Norway controls the north. They could have gone west, though.

Down the valley of Loch Ness and out Loch Linne to the Isle of Mull. Then sail to Ireland."

No, thought Mary, Donalbain is the one going to Ireland.

"But why would anybody *want* to go to Ireland?" Fleance mused. "I bet they headed for the pass at Drumochter and went south to England."

Scotland was a country sliced in the sides with rivers and bays, cluttered in the middle with mountains. South were the Grampians, rough and steep. "There are only a few passes," Mary pointed out, "and they'll be guarded. Patrols will cut the princes off or cut them down."

Fleance gave that some thought. Mary could not imagine how he had managed to kill Asleif. He had no more force than a butterfly. He had not even tried to get back the brooch, whose gold was valuable, and whose existence was proof of his kill.

"I don't know about that," said Fleance slowly. "Men loved Duncan. They would love his sons, too. Of course, kings don't like king killers, so I shouldn't think the King of England would take them in."

Unless the King of England thinks the princes are innocent, thought Mary. She did not meet Fleance's eyes. She feared that they did indeed have the same thought.

If Malcolm and Donalbain had not killed the King, only one other person was likely to have done it.

The new king.

Tell me, thou unknown power . . .
ACT IV, SCENE 1

INCE FORRES WAS A PALACE AND SURELY HAD ITS OWN STAFF, Swin was stunned to learn that they all had to go – she and Jennet and Fhiora and Rousay and everyone else who lived and worked at Inverness.

How would her grandfather survive? She wanted to beg Lady Macbeth – the Queen, rather – to let her stay, but others born at Inverness with family here had tried and failed. Swin had no better arguments than they did.

"Why do we all have to go?" she asked Ildred. Until now, Swin had always known more than Ildred. Suddenly, their positions were reversed.

"She wants a huge court," said Ildred. "Troops of friends. Glory and honor."

"I'm a scullery maid," said Swin. "I'm not the court, or a friend, and I won't bring glory and honor."

Ildred laughed. Swin had not heard Ildred laugh in years. It made her pretty and young. She was thinner now, too, the babe having been born, and her recovery going well.

Swin almost said that she knew, that all the kitchen girls knew. She almost said that the reason she had talked of the babe in front of Ildred was to make sure Ildred knew that Father Ninian had buried the baby with love. She had even beaten up Fhiora to keep her from adding details Ildred did not need.

But Ildred would be heartsick if she found out that they all knew, so Swin said nothing and set out for the last time to see her grandfather. It was a large haul, because the confusion of packing and the carrying of large bags everywhere had made it much easier to gather things.

It was dark again today, and chilly, with a wind that came and went like an evil spirit. Swin wanted to run and feared to run, wanted to be out of sight of the castle and feared to be. In the woods, vines had grown up, and their little tips of leaf and tangle kept reaching for her hair. She kept hearing things, things as had no name, things as crept and crawled and killed.

She stopped only a hundred yards into the trees, a quarter mile and two brooks away from the path that led to her grandfather.

I who live by the knife, thought Swin, did not bring a knife.

She looked around. She could hear nothing, see nothing, yet was filled with dread.

She set down the pack and the bag, moved vines over them, and immediately the brown leather was a stump or a stone. Even Swin would have a hard time finding them when she came back. She walked carefully away from the food and away from the path that led to her grandfather. Strong fingers clamped around her wrist. "Swin, Swin. Stealing around in the forest? Or just stealing?"

She turned slowly, although she knew it was Seyton. "I'm getting berries for the Queen's dinner."

"I don't see any berries here."

"Nor do I."

"Where's your pack?" demanded Seyton.

"Pack?" said Swin. She was fairly sure she could beat him to a pulp. But no matter how strong she was, in the law of the land, he was stronger. She would be hanged for attacking a noble.

"I saw you sneak away," he said.

"Sneak?" she repeated. What power had stopped her from going close to the path? What power had ensured that Seyton would not find the way to her grandfather's hut?

She said *Thank you* in her heart, and walked away from Seyton, back to the castle. If he had caught her with stolen food, he would not have turned her in for punishment. He would save her, to use later. And what could Swin do for him that he might need?

Swin, who was good with a knife and not afraid of blood?

. . . these terrible dreams
That shake us nightly.
ACT III, SCENE 2

T HE FINAL NIGHT AT INVERNESS THERE WAS A PARTY FOR THE departing Queen, and the hall rang with laughter and song. And then, for everyone but the Queen, a long, hard night because the beds were packed on carts.

Mary pitied Ildred, on clean rushes near the ladies-in-waiting, who kept giving her orders. She could not join Swin and Jennet and Rousay and Fhiora, who lay beside one another in the kitchen.

Mary used her heavy felted cloak with its roomy hood for her bedding and the pack that had been Donalbain's (or Malcolm's) for a pillow. She slept on the floor of the chapel, or tried.

Sleep would not come.

Mary dreaded the visit to Cawdor, yet ached for it. She wanted the Queen to call her by name but feared being noticed. When at last she slept, she dreamed that she was showing off the secret passage at Cawdor, and they locked her in there. The nightmare wrenched her awake. Her heart was still violently pounding when she heard footsteps as light as a cat's. If it was a cat, Mary didn't mind. But it was not likely to be a cat. Not in the murder-haunted, dead-light dark castle.

Even more extraordinary than Mary's worst fears, it was Lady Macbeth.

The Queen held a candle stuck lopsidedly into an old wooden base that was layered with drippings. She walked at the same angle as her candle, as if she had tilted at some point and gotten one leg shorter than the other. Her hair had fallen out of her cap, and the cap had fallen on her shoulder. The flickering light exaggerated the Queen's features, turning the circles under her eyes to craters.

Lady Macbeth set the candle down rather slowly on the altar, as if she had lost understanding of how to let go of things. Yet she did not look down and she did not look up, but straight across — at nothing. It was cold, and the Queen began to rub her hands together to warm them. "Don't look so pale!" she snapped.

Mary started to apologize.

But the Queen was not addressing Mary. "I keep telling you,

my love," she said to thin air. "Duncan is dead. He can't get out of the grave."

Mary could not see the person the Queen was talking to.

The Queen rubbed her hands again. "Out!" she ordered her skin. And irritably, like a housemaid with a task she cannot finish, "Damned spot."

Mary had never heard the Queen swear.

"Who would have thought the old man had so much blood in him?" said Lady Macbeth. She lifted her hand and sniffed her palm. "It still smells of blood. All the perfumes of Arabia will not sweeten this little hand."

Swin stank of blood when she slaughtered a sheep. Sometimes she was standing in it, her wooden shoes sopping it up. It was a horrid coppery smell that made Mary gag.

"Enough blood," murmured the Queen, "to paint the pillows of those servants. Now they'll look guilty." Lady Macbeth turned and shuffled out of the chapel. She forgot her candle.

Mary had heard of sleepwalking but never seen it.

In a dream, you did not choose the sequence or the story. Things happened that were not real nor were you really there.

Was this a walking dream, in which the Queen of Scotland had not been there and it had not happened?

Or was it a confession of murder?

How now, you secret, black, and midnight hags?
ACT IV, SCENE 1

L ADY MACBETH'S TRAIN DID NOT, AFTER ALL, STOP AT CAWDOR. Where the stone shaft marked the turn, they did not pause. Cart after cart drew drearily through the mud. Every head was bent, every face shielded, in the vain hope of avoiding the pelting rain. Mary turned her pony and rode toward Cawdor.

Exultation filled her. Cawdor wasn't hers, her parents were dead, the castle was empty – but she was going home.

She was so happy when she came up and over the last hill. Now the towers of Cawdor would loom against the sky. Mary flung back her hood and whooped with joy.

But Cawdor was not there.

It had to be here. She had grown up here. She knew these fields. She had waded in that burn, hunted foxes in that glen. It must be over the next hill, then.

But it wasn't.

She rode on and on, thinking – It must be here! – beyond that marsh! – behind those trees!

And it wasn't.

It seemed to Mary that the sky ceased to record time. There was neither day nor night, east nor west: just the endless heath, rain, and chill.

A cat mewed. Three times.

There came a muffled bang and the slosh of water.

"Three times I stir my cauldron," said a voice she had heard before. "Double, double, toil and trouble. Fire burn cauldron bubble."

In front of Mary stood the Weird Ones, half melted from their own fire, their hair and fingernails dripping at the ends. "This night we'll spend," they crooned, "for a fatal end. Upon the corner of the moon, there hangs −"

They saw Mary. They smiled. They beckoned.

"Fillet of a fenny snake in the cauldron boil and bake." They pointed down into their brew. "Scale of dragon, tooth of wolf."

Many found that she had dismounted. That her pony was trotting away. That her feet were carrying her toward the curly fingers of the laughing witches.

"Girl-child of a thane we take, down inside the cauldron stake."

And now about the cauldron sing
Like elves and fairies in a ring,
Enchanting all that you put in.
ACT IV, SCENE 1

FAR OFF, THE RAIN STOPPED.

Fleance could see it like a tear in fabric.

A golden haze shone in a far valley. Fleance saw a small white house and a distant red door. Between him and the cottage, a field was pink with heather and beyond that rose the crisp strength of pines. And Lady Mary, riding toward the sun.

His father, Banquo, was far ahead, rounding a bend and disappearing from sight. The Queen in her covered carriage with her ladies followed him.

Lady Mary had been lucky so far. First King Duncan had forgotten about her and then so had the Macbeths. If her luck held, she would just slide into the new court with some minor task and be married off to some minor functionary. If her luck did not hold . . .

She must not run, he thought. It'll look as if she is planning treachery, like her father before her. All the things they let go — like those witnesses who heard her pray for Cawdor and Macdonwald — they won't let that go after all.

Fleance clucked to his horse and followed her.

The countryside was filled with stone crosses carved like lace. They reminded God to protect the passerby. Fleance studied the one where Mary had turned off. Its slender arrow pointed to Cawdor.

Mary had gone over a hill, and Fleance rode faster, lest he lose her.

He could smell the sea and hear the breakers, but he could not see the castle. In fact, he could not find the sea. The day tried to distract him. Red grouse burst up, whirring their wings like the rolled *r* of his speech.

But no Lady Mary.

And then the day went bad, a filthy fog creeping up around him, and the smell of decay kicked up with the mud. In front of him, oozing out of the fog, were three men – or were they women? Women with beards? The clothes they wore seemed attached to the earth, and behind them, tongues of orange flame licked the bottom of a great pot. A cat cried, and Fleance's horse stopped short and would move no closer. The creatures were laughing, as if they had won something. Or gloating, as if they had caught something. Behind them, struggling, trying to pull free, Fleance thought for a moment he saw Mary of Shiel. And he did not really see anything, only fog and filth.

But he went to her rescue even when she might not be there, leaping off his horse and catapulting his scrawny self on the three weaving, wailing women.

But they were not there. The soil bubbled, and they were gone, and Mary of Shiel held out her arms.

This is what it is to be loved, thought Fleance. A girl holds out her arms.

He lost sight of the creatures. He forgot them, in fact. The stench and the fog and the fire evaporated from his mind as they had from the soil.

For a moment as long as tide – that moment of peace where tide is neither in nor out, just before the water changes its mind and rushes back the way it came – he held her to his chest.

And his great love, sharp as his spur, hath holp him . . .
ACT I, SCENE 6

M ARY HAD THOUGHT IT WAS HER FATHER, COME TO RESCUE her and take her home. She had thought it was her father when he was young. She had thought he would swing her on his shoulder and carry her like his princess and all would be well.

Fleance.

How wicked to be in debt to the one who killed your true love.

And how astonishing that poor, silly Fleance, forgetting he had a sword and steel, flew to her rescue with bare fists and without a thought for his own safety. Asleif had been like that.

Mary's eyes had somehow opened too wide. She could not close them. They no longer protected her thought, no longer veiled her soul, but were open doors. Other people would see in where as normally Mary saw out.

I interrupted the Weird Ones, she thought. I saw what mortals may not see. They have altered my sight.

Under the soles of her thin leather boots, she felt the Weird Ones moving.

Up through the grass came their strange cold voices, like mourners in a stony place.

Pony with a crooked star
Runs a ride that goes too far.
The owl wins against the wren,
the hollow tree a pen for men.

"What does it mean?" she whispered, gripping Fleance hard, so that they could not pull her down with them.

"What does what mean?" asked Fleance.

CHAPTER 9

Confusion now hath made his masterpiece!
ACT II, SCENE 3

THE GREAT HALL AT CASTLE FORRES WAS PAINTED WHITE. CENTERED in each huge rectangular stone was a bright flower or prancing unicorn. Sunlight poured through second-story windows, reflected on the white walls, and gave the room such brilliance. Rafters were draped with banners. Tapestries hung here and there, each one a battle scene.

"We will design our own tapestry," said the new queen, "of our husband's victory over the traitor Macdonwald on the sands of Moray."

The ladies-in-waiting did indeed wait, eager to hear the Queen praise the brave contributions of their husbands, brothers, and fathers. But the Queen did not even seem to recall that King Duncan and Banquo had been part of that victory, let alone other lesser men. Mary yearned to remind her. The Queen could remove her ladies' disappointment with one gracious smile, one kind word. But who was Mary to correct a queen?

The Queen explored her new home. She swept through side rooms and sitting rooms and even storerooms. Crowds eager to see their new queen thronged the rooms and the halls, swarmed up the stairs, and clotted in the doorways. Servants were everywhere. Forres had a separate staff for pantry, larder, buttery, kitchen, kennel, and laundry. It had a candle maker, coffin maker, brewer, barber, beverage keeper, and wardrobe steward.

Lady Macbeth loved having so many at her beck and call. And beckon she did, gesturing with her head or hand to summon or demand. She did not bother with speech, forcing each man or woman to guess what was wanted and to bring it before the Queen had to utter a syllable.

The party was going up the stairs on the western wall when Fleance said to Mary, "Don't go that way. Come with me."

She didn't bother to reply.

"Please trust me," said Fleance.

To think that Mary had been rescued by the man who killed Asleif. To think she was actually calling Fleance a man!

Fleance had rounded up her pony, helped her mount, held the pony's reins, and led her back to the caravan, while she sat in a fog of her own, unable to fathom why she had not found Cawdor.

Where *had* Cawdor gone? Or was it Mary who had gone some-where? To some realm that did not exist?

And the Weird Ones, from whom Fleance had saved her, but whose songs he had not heard. *The owl wins against the wren.* Owls were dreadful creatures, swooping down in the dark, ripping to pieces their tiny prey, casually sitting on some low branch to nibble a head or tail. What had that meant? Why had she heard it?

Fleance said gently, "They've put the heads of the traitors on spikes on the west wall. You must not look."

Her father's head. After so much time. Such bad weather. So many pecking birds.

Mary swallowed the bile of horror in her throat. Fleance had saved her a second time. She had called him a butterfly in her thoughts. But he was watchful. He was kind.

Why had no one else tried to be kind? They didn't know about the west wall, Mary told herself. And my queen – she doesn't know. Or she would have warned me.

"Come up these stairs with me instead," said Fleance. "The ladies will soon reach the chapel, and you can rejoin them there."

The stairs wound tightly around a central core, each step treacherously narrow at the center but opening to a wide and gracious wedge at the outer wall. Sure enough, at the top Mary found the ladies swirling out of the other gallery and coming this way.

"Dear Eglantyne," the Queen was saying. Mary loved that name. Eglantyne was a kind of rose, and this lady-in-waiting *was* a rose – so fair, with such pink cheeks and yellow hair. "Is not this castle beautiful, Eglantyne?" asked the Queen, whose smile was different these days, smaller and tighter. "Perfect in every way?"

Lady Eglantyne bowed. "Perfection is what you deserve, my queen."

Mary clapped with the rest.

The chapel, on the second floor, was above the solid protective walls and could have a window. It was flooded with light. The stained glass was vivid – green and red, sun yellow and cobalt blue. Mary could have stared forever at Jesus feeding the five thousand. But the altar was covered with dust. Even if King Duncan had taken the priest to war with him, the priest should be here now. He or his altar boys should be keeping the chapel sparkling clean.

And where was Father Ninian? Mary had not seen him. In fact, she suddenly realized there had been no mass today, and no mass during the journey, either. No prayers at all. As if the new king and queen had shrugged off God.

The Queen swept on. Her gown had a remarkably long skirt, trailing behind her like a velvet waterfall. The ladies watched carefully not to step on it. Since Mary had not actually been invited to join them, it was easy to linger behind. She found the steward, who did not seem happy to talk about the priest of Forres. Finally, he said, "Our priest tutored the princes, you know. Taught Malcolm and Donalbain their Latin and their reading. He loved them." The steward thought about this for a while, and then he walked off.

If this priest had truly loved Malcolm and Donalbain, perhaps he went to England himself to find them, thought Mary. But if he thought the princes really *had* murdered their father, would he follow them to a far country? Surely not.

Mary found the almoner, the palace officer charged with bringing royal help to the poor. It was his task to visit the sick, the lepers, the widows, and the crippled. He had just emptied a purse of coins into his palm and was counting them. Mary was pleased that so many would have help. "Have you seen Father Ninian, our priest?" she asked. "He's very old and bent, with white hair and a trembly voice."

"I have not seen such a person."

"But who will say mass? Who will hear confession?"

The almoner stared at the coins in his hand. "Indeed," said the almoner softly, "a priest does hear confession, doesn't he? Perhaps someone confessed something."

Mary's thumbs pricked.

There was but one truly evil thing a man might have confessed: Duncan's murder. It could not have been Malcolm or Donalbain confessing – they ran too soon to speak to Father Ninian.

If Macbeth had done the murder, would he confess? No, because he would not think it was a sin to fulfill his destiny. But what if Father Ninian guessed what everyone else was guessing? What if the old priest accused the new king – Macbeth was a member of his flock, after all – of murder? Would Macbeth have thrown him out? Or done something even worse? A man who dared kill a king would not stop at killing a mere parish priest.

Or had some other murderer confessed and regretted telling anyone? And left Father Ninian dead in some wild place, to be chewed by foxes?

The almoner also walked away from Mary.

Father Ninian is fine, she told herself. He wasn't strong enough for the journey and I wasn't thoughtful enough to check on him. He made the wise decision to stay where he was and conserve his strength for the Lord.

Those he commands move only in command,
Nothing in love.
ACT V, SCENE 2

I LDRED WAS AIRING THE GOWNS OF DUNCAN'S LONG-DEAD QUEEN IN a solar so spacious that a dozen women could stitch a dozen projects here. She draped each lovely dress over a couch or a window seat.

The King was back from Scone, and a feast had been announced. The Queen had in mind to give a finer feast than Duncan ever gave and for a finer king: her own Macbeth — whose subjects did not rebel and whose servants and sons did not commit murder.

It was time to choose the gown the new queen would wear for the occasion.

The ladies-in-waiting rushed into the solar like little waves at high tide, burbling and foaming with delight at being near the new queen.

How did people acquire these troops of friends? Where did they come from? Why could Ildred never find even one friend?

"All colors flatter you," said one of the ladies, "but this dark crimson, with the white ermine trim! So regal! So queenly!"

Ildred thought it looked like the color of dried blood.

"Perfect!" chorused the ladies, laughing and clapping.

At the bottom of a chest, Ildred had found a real crown, thick and gold. In the very center was one fine pearl, round and smooth and shimmering. Ildred lifted the crown by her fingertips for the Queen to admire. But the Queen frowned. "My diamond was nicer. Ildred, where is my diamond?"

Ildred wanted to say, *You threw it away.* But she said politely, "I never found it, your highness."

Lady Macbeth's eyes rested on Ildred with no more friendship in them than Swin bestowed on a soon-to-be-dinner sheep. Five years of my life, thought Ildred, fawning on her and serving her, and I am nothing to her.

"What diamond was that, your highness?" asked Eglantyne.

Eglantyne and Ildred had grown up together, their fathers good friends, their lands adjoining. It was a canker on Ildred's heart to see Eglantyne being the rosy-cheeked lady-in-waiting, while she, Ildred, was just a servant who couldn't keep track of the Queen's jewels.

"A gift from good King Duncan. Ildred lost it." She turned her back on Ildred.

Eglantyne shot Ildred a look of compassion. Lady Ross nodded meaningfully at Ildred, as if saying, *I will solve this.*

But there was no solution. The diamond, whatever had happened to it, was at Inverness. Ildred could not imagine where it had gone. Could Swin have curled her long bare toes around it and dropped it into her wooden shoe to sell later? But Swin had not been on that side of the room, so unless the diamond bounced back across the entire kitchen, this was not the answer. Or was Swin right, and dead-lights had sticky fingers?

"At the feast tonight," said the new queen, "we will have all our dear friends. My lord King Macbeth and all who went with him to Scone are here at last, and of course we have all those who stayed behind, such as dear old Banquo, so good at handling baggage and such."

The ladies were silent.

They're not dear friends, thought Ildred. They're subjects. It isn't the same.

Our fears in Banquo.
Stick deep . . .
ACT III, SCENE 1

MARY HAD NO ASSIGNMENT FOR THE BANQUET. ALLIES WERE being made, friendships cemented. But the daughter of Cawdor had no place in such things.

She peeked in the Great Hall, where servants were preparing for the feast.

Stacked on the steps that went up to the dais where the royal party would dine were the guest gifts. Mary recognized them.

The gold and silver vessels of her father's table service. Others had found Cawdor where it was supposed to be.

Tonight, when they hand out things that were once mine, thought Mary, they will announce what is to happen to me.

Mary went outdoors. She felt safer, somehow, where the air was fresh. But it smelled of low tide, damp and brackish. She filled her lungs with salt and choked. She thought of the Weird Ones, whose grip she had been unable to break, and how, at the touch of Fleance, they had melted.

Best to think of earthly things. Mary looked around. There stood the King. Oh, but Macbeth was regal! So tall and brawny, so dark of hair and eye! Then she saw his face.

The King was snarling like a hound closing in on a deer. His lips curled back, and his strong white teeth were exposed, ready to clamp down on some thin bone and shatter it. Thank God Macbeth wasn't staring at her that way. Who would Macbeth rather bite than look at?

Banquo.

The Queen had dismissed Banquo as a pleasant man good at moving possessions. There was some truth to that. He was no Lord Macduff, who controlled Fife and owned so many castles. No Lord Ross, with a county to call his own and a rich, landed wife. No Lennox, with ancestors so impressive. He was just Banquo, busy as always with Fleance at his side.

Banquo walked off to consult with some official, who nodded and frowned. Fleance stayed where he was. Macbeth's gaze did not follow Banquo. The snarl moved on and off his face like a wasp deciding where to sting.

Mary's thumbs pricked. It was not Banquo whom Macbeth hated. It was Fleance.

⸻

. . . it must be done tonight . . .
ACT III, SCENE 1

⸻

FLEANCE," SAID HIS FATHER SHARPLY. "COME. WE'RE LEAVING. DON'T bring anything with you." He marched Fleance into the courtyard, where a stable hand had their horses ready. His father mounted, but Fleance spotted Macduff and had to shout hello to one of his favorite people on earth.

Macduff barreled right over. Big in the chest, with muscles to match, his skinny legs looked like yellow fence posts in the fashionable hose he had chosen. Macduff loved to laugh, and even his laugh was like something pouring from a barrel, infectious and full of froth. "My friends!" called Macduff, already laughing. "Where are you off to so late in the afternoon? We have a solemn supper tonight, remember."

His father did not answer but kept his muscles taut with readiness. Ready for what?

"We'll be there," Fleance promised. "How were your chicks? How was your visit to Fife? It's good to see you back from Fife, sir."

Macduff had time only to grin when the King appeared, striding toward them. Macbeth was every inch the king, and he knew it. It was a pleasure to watch the man.

Banquo dismounted and bowed.

Fleance himself forgot to bow. He was a boy who watched kings and captains; he wasn't one of them or part of it.

"Banquo!" cried Macbeth, in a huge hearty voice, as if the sight of his old friend was utterly unexpected. "But what is this? Where are you off to? We have a feast tonight, remember. We celebrate the joy of our new world – and somewhat less pleasantly, we have to decide what to do about those murdering sons of Duncan."

Banquo bowed so low his face could not be seen. "Let your highness command me."

The King smiled. "My command is simple. Return in time for dinner." His eyes swung over Fleance. "Your son goes with you?"

Too late, Fleance thought of bowing. Embarrassment made his bow even more awkward than usual. His knees seem to have multiplied and his brains to have abandoned him. His father sounded careful, like a diplomat not sure what was coming. "He does, sire."

"May your horses be swift and sure of foot," said the King.

It was a lovely benediction. Fleance smiled.

. . . and with him,
To leave no rubs nor botches in the work,
Fleance his son, that keeps him company . . .
ACT III, SCENE 1

Y OU ARE NEEDED," SAID MACBETH.

It was the sentence Seyton had waited to hear all his life. "I am your servant."

"A piece of work lies before us."

Seyton thrilled to the word *us*.

"I have an enemy. His name, as you said, blisters my tongue."

Seyton nodded.

"Arrangements have been made. I am, however, unsure. I need a third man."

Seyton did not want to be third. He wanted to be first. But that would come. He would prove himself. "What is your gracious pleasure, highness?"

Thou hast it now — King, Cawdor, Glamis, all,
As the Weird Women promised; and I fear
Thou played most foully for it.

ACT III, SCENE 1

THEY WERE HARDLY OUT OF SIGHT OF FORRES WHEN BANQUO began to lecture Fleance. "Some men, my son," he said, "are greyhounds. Many are mongrels or wolves. A few are spaniels. Macbeth is a cur."

"Father!"

"He murdered Duncan with his own hands and hid his crime by slaughtering those innocent servants." Banquo spurred his horse. "We have much territory to cover, Fleance, and little time."

"What are we doing?"

"We're doing what Malcolm and Donalbain did. We're running."

"*We're running?* Father, we can't! We must turn around and get back for that feast."

Banquo went faster.

"Father, what about our pledge of loyalty?"

"Our loyalty is to our rightful king, and that is dead Duncan, and that means our loyalty is to the heir Duncan named, and that is Malcolm."

"Father! If we're not at this feast, people will think we're traitors, too!"

"Malcolm and Donalbain are no traitors. They ran so they would not be murdered," said Banquo, "and that is why you and I are running."

Fleance was horrified. Banquo and Fleance and every other noble had pledged loyalty to Macbeth! Their entire future lay in that court! They could not go to England or Ireland or hide out in some bog! "Father, nobody wants to murder us."

"Macbeth and I were stopped on the heath by three witches who told us the future. They said that Macbeth would become Cawdor, and after that, he would become king. We laughed, but what they said came true. *In hours.*"

His father pulled up. Fleance reined in, too. "Listen to me!" Banquo gripped his son's wrist, tightening his fingers as if to crunch the bones. "The witches said that no child of Macbeth would be king after him. They said *my* issue would produce the kings. Macbeth had a smoking sword on that battlefield, and he had knives in that bedroom, but he doesn't have sons. *I have the son.*"

"Father, this is crazy. We have to go back. We still have time. It's a feast to celebrate his coronation."

"There's nothing to celebrate. Macbeth and that evil wife of his are in this together."

"They are not, Father! No sweet woman would think of such things as you imply."

"Think, Fleance. If Macbeth has no sons, and if my son is to rule after him, *who must be murdered next?*"

Fleance meditated. *Me?* he thought. *I* have to be murdered next?

But in that awful list of dogs, Fleance was afraid that he himself might be a spaniel. Pleasant enough, but no leader of the pack. Macbeth — no cur, in Fleance's opinion, but certainly a savage hound — would not bother with Fleance.

Perhaps it was not Fleance himself in that prophecy, but *his* sons who were to rule. That meant Fleance would have to marry and have children.

Marriage made him think of Lady Mary, which made him blush. Why could he not have told the truth about the dead man on the sand? Why had he let Seyton pay false compliments? Forevermore Lady Mary would see Fleance as the killer of her loved one. He could at least have pretended to kill somebody who didn't matter to Lady Mary.

He thought of that brief embrace and her careful avoidance of him ever since.

He forgot to think of murder.

THE GREAT HALL WAS CHAOTIC AND FULL OF EXCITEMENT.
Dinner was usually at noon, while supper was a light meal taken rather early. But a feast started late and ended late. How rare and splendid to have every torch lit, every corner bright!

Everyone was in the Great Hall, unwilling to miss a moment.

Acrobats tumbled and spun. Jugglers practiced. On a projecting balcony, musicians had tuned their viols and were absently plucking their harps. Serving boys ran to fill cups, and from the kitchen passage came the savory smells of roasting meat and baking bread. Throngs of men waited to see the King.

Lady Ross and the Queen were playing chess. Lady Ross could whip Mary and Eglantyne and everybody else at chess. She was letting the Queen win, and everyone but the Queen knew it.

The Queen had not chosen the dark crimson gown after all but a rich deep-purple gown whose lace collar stood up like feathers. She was beautiful. And when gentlemen came up to her, and bent a knee, and kissed her hand, and paid her compliments, the Queen handled her new office as if she had practiced for it.

They had said that of Mary's father, when he was facing execution.

I forgot him, thought Mary. So much has happened with such speed that my heart and mind cannot keep up.

Macbeth strode in. His boots were high, with hard heels, and he stamped over the great polished stone floor of the hall, so much more regal than wading over soft and rotting rushes. He had chosen a tunic of black, crosshatched in red, but his cape the opposite: red trimmed in black. How dark, thick, and curly were his hair and beard, how strong and cheerful his voice!

The ladies jumped up and patted their hair, ducked their eyes, and made long, swooping curtsies. He gave them what they sought: a moment's attention and compliments on how lovely they looked.

Up went the score of long, narrow tables, with their long, narrow benches. The dais was high. Everybody would have the pleasure of feasting their eyes as well as their bodies – studying the new king, admiring the new queen, and especially seeing who was sitting next to whom, for in this a man's future could be read.

The King and Queen spoke low to each other, and then she lifted her skirts and stepped up on the dais. She stroked the beautifully carved arms of her ancient chair and settled on the puffy cushion, nestling into the sheer pleasure of being queen. Her ladies found their places, and one by one the nobles and lesser guests looked for theirs.

But the meal was not served because the King did not sit.

He drifted away – if a king can drift.

Everyone was waiting. It was a curious, shivery thing – a king was present, and yet everyone was waiting.

For what? For whom?

Now spurs the lated traveler apace
To gain the timely inn . . .
ACT III, SCENE 3

W E'RE RIDING THE SAME ROAD, THOUGHT FLEANCE, OVER which the princes fled and the King's men followed. The same road Macbeth took to his crowning at Scone. The country people are rolling their eyes and saying, 'Here they come again.' And now the King's men will be sent after Father and me, and there will be a price on *our* heads. What if we don't find Malcolm? I don't want to serve the King of England.

It was growing dark.

They rode on and on, as if Banquo had no plan to stop until they reached England. Finally, his father said, "There's an inn at the foot of that hill."

In the pitch dark, Fleance couldn't even see the hill.

"We stop there for the night," said his father. "By the time the King and his devil wife realize we're not coming back, it will be too late for them to follow us. We'll be safe before they can catch up. The important thing is your life." His father smiled at Fleance, a rare thing. "No matter what happens, dear son, your life is more precious than mine."

Fleance could not smile back. He was appalled by what they were doing. Running was a low act. He thought less of Malcolm and Donalbain for running. Even if they had a good reason, kings didn't run. Who wanted Malcolm for king anyhow if his first act was to run?

Several hundred yards ahead, a single yellow lamp glowed. Fleance began to think of supper and sleep. Banquo rode faster, but Fleance let his horse amble. His eyes closed. He wasn't a good enough rider to doze in the saddle so he woke himself up, and saw that the very shadows where his father rode were leaping and growling.

"Fleance!" screamed Banquo, his horse rearing and kicking, bringing sharp hoofs down on a high, round shape. A hooded man. They were being robbed.

"Run!" bellowed his father.

It was the thing Fleance most did not want to do. So he didn't. Beginning now, Fleance must be the savage hound that tore the enemy to pieces. He slid off his horse, dirk out. It would have been faster and better to ride up close, but on the beach he hadn't managed to fight from the saddle.

He could see three attackers now, two in the leather jerkins of peasants and one in armor. They had battle-axes. Fleance was dumbfounded. Robbers robbed; they didn't start wars. His father was still alive only because his horse was wild with fear, long legs tangling like vines with swinging blades. Fleance came up behind one robber and hurled his entire body weight behind his dirk. The man wore a large cloak, and exactly where his flesh lay inside that cloak, Fleance could not tell. He prayed to hit vitals, pierce lung or heart or spine. But the dirk went easily through the flesh of the man's side, and with a howl of rage and pain, the robber twisted away. The dirk remained in him. Fleance lost his grip on his only weapon. Hands were no match for three battle-axes.

The robber swung wildly with the ax, hoping to cleave Fleance in two, as Macbeth on a battlefield had ended the life of Macdonwald. But Fleance leaped clear, and the ax hit the soil with a sickening thud. Fleance flashed forward to take back the knife.

He saw his father, down and half-dead. Fleance attacked the robber about to deal the deathblow to Banquo. It was the man in armor. Fleance was puzzled by the armor — a robber on the moor had a noble's gear? — but he slashed as viciously as he could and had the satisfaction of seeing blood spurt from the forearm of the attacker.

The battle-ax swung anyway. Fleance leaped back, saving his skin but not his knife. It was knocked from his hand. A second time, he was weaponless.

A battle-ax came down yet again upon his father. Yet even in dying, his father found the strength for one last cry. "Save yourself, my son! Because I love you! I order it!"

Had the word *love* not been used, Fleance would have died gladly at his father's side, hoping he could take down at least one of these murderers. But he knew the truth of his father's love, and he knew that the only gift he could give his father now was to live. He veered into the wood.

But perhaps he had done the wrong thing. For Banquo shouted one more word before the battle-axes came down for the last time. "Slave!" he bellowed.

The worst insult a man could deliver. With his dying breath, had Banquo called his own son a slave?

Was the hope drunk
Wherein you dressed yourself?
ACT I, SCENE 7

SWIN WAS IMPRESSED.

When somebody finally said grace, the pantrymen brought in the first course of bread and butter – six kinds of bread! prettily decorated tubs of butter! – while the beverage men toted in the ale and wine. Then came a barley and leek soup tastier than anything Swin had ever thrown together, and venison stew in huge bowls with huge ladles.

She loved all the light. Beautiful wall sconces held torches burning bright, throwing soot against the white-painted walls and the yellow flowers. She hoped she wouldn't be scrubbing it off. Tables had candlesticks, some holding one candle, some three, or even nine. The log in the hearth was the size of an ox, giving off a wonderful heat. The palace needed heat. Its stone walls were eight feet thick.

How Swin admired the dessert. It was a rarity: rice pudding! She had watched them make it, with dozens of eggs, buckets of cream, with sugar and cinnamon, ginger and mace. She yearned for a taste. All the staff yearned for a taste. But it had not been made for them. Swin didn't even get to lick out a bowl because it wasn't her kitchen.

She counted the puddings. Exactly the right number to serve the seated guests. There would be no pilfering here.

What would become of her grandfather when food ran out?

She wished she could talk to Father Ninian. Where was he, anyway? And Dirle. What had happened to Ildred's dog? He wasn't here. Usually Ildred searched for him twice a day. Why wasn't she moaning and poking around, trying to find Dirle?

The King had not yet seated himself. His casual wandering around the room, chatting here, laughing there, clapping a friend on the shoulder, greeting a newcomer – it had gone on too long. Why was Macbeth not joining the feast?

Swin had the oddest thought. The man was afraid of his own throne.

As from your graves rise up . . .
ACT II, SCENE 3

MARY'S THUMBS WERE BEING BITTEN BY A SERPENT. SHE PRESSED them against the underside of the table, hoping the pain would enter the wood, but it only grew worse.

She was at a low table again, which was fine, because the last thing she wanted was to attract notice. But every table and every guest had a fine view of the dais, and the empty chair where the King continued not to sit.

How murky were the white walls behind that chair. How the

smoke from the hearth swirled there, and roosted, and collected. The seat of the king's chair was higher than anyone else's. It had a wooden canopy, finely carved, and a thick cushion, beautifully woven. The sooty shadows thickened and flickered over the chair, as if some small black Macbeth was trying to sit down.

The pricking in her thumbs moved up into her palms and down her wrists, on the march toward her heart.

The shadow on the royal seat became Banquo, who had come at last, just as he had promised.

On Banquo's right, the Queen, her lady Macbeth, said nothing.

On Banquo's left, Lord Lennox patted the chair where Banquo sat. His hand went through Banquo. "Come, my lord king," he called to Macbeth. "Sit. Please."

The King seemed puzzled. "Where?" he said.

A hundred men looked up. Where else would the King sit except his royal seat?

After a moment of confusion, Lord Ross stood up and walked over to the King to escort him.

The King did not move even with the pressure of Ross's hand on his arm.

Mary looked back at the chair. Banquo was still there. He had acquired color and form. But he did not breathe.

Banquo, dead and drenched in blood, sat in the seat of the King.

CHAPTER 10

Fair and noble hostess,
We are your guest tonight.
ACT I, SCENE 6

HEAR THE RUMORS?" SAID THE MAN NEXT TO MARY. "THEY SAY Prince Malcolm reached England, and Donalbain's in Ireland."

Mary was looking all the way through Banquo. His dead body wavered and shifted like a reflection in a pool.

"Is it not strange?" asked the man. "Brothers who commit a murder, you'd think they would stay together. Maybe they fell out with each other, too."

Mary pointed to bleeding, shuddering Banquo, and her table

companion smiled and said, "Look! Here comes the lamb and gravy."

Huge platters were balanced on the shoulders and fingertips of a dozen servants.

"If only Banquo were here," said the King. "He said he'd be back for my feast."

On the throne, Banquo twitched and bled.

Mary hung so tightly to the table she felt nailed to it.

Lord Ross tried to maneuver the King to the dais. "Please grace us with your company, sir."

And the King – the King of Scotland! – lord of this palace! – said, "There's nowhere to sit. All the seats are full."

Lord Lennox patted the chair where Banquo was sitting. "Right here, sir. Next to me."

Banquo did not feel Lennox.

Lennox did not feel Banquo.

Mary pressed her white napkin against her mouth.

Dead Banquo shook his head. Drops of blood spattered so far and wide that Mary ducked – yet on the pure white tablecloth, not one red splash appeared.

Macbeth had seen it, too. "How did you get here?" he shouted at Banquo. "You're not alive!"

Banquo grinned savagely.

"Don't you shake your bloody head at me!" shrieked Macbeth.

Servants pouring ale missed the cups. Fingers holding meat paused midair. Voices having conversations stopped midword.

Banquo's dead, thought Mary. That's why the blood doesn't stain. He's a ghost.

Macbeth spoke as if he and Banquo were alone in the room. "You cannot say I did it!"

Banquo is dead, thought Mary, and Fleance, who is always at his side, rode off with his father this afternoon.

Ross loyally tried to handle the King's behavior. "Gentlemen, I fear his majesty is unwell. Shall we depart and let him rest?"

"No!" cried the Queen.

Mary had forgotten the Queen. Now she saw a thin, nervous stranger, wringing her hands, furious and afraid. "Please, dear friends, keep your seats," she said, trying to rescue her banquet.

So much repeats itself, thought Mary. Two rebels against a king. Two battlefields. Two servants murdered. Two feasts ruined.

"This fit will last but a moment," said the Queen. "He has had these seizures since his youth," she added desperately. Since every man here had known Macbeth since his youth, they were skeptical of her claim. "Let me talk to him for a moment, and all will be well," she assured her guests, patting their shoulders as she squeezed by, rushing to her husband's side. "Eat!" she called cheerily. "Drink! Be merry!" She swept her husband away from the high table and into the gallery beneath the musicians.

Some ate. Some drank. Most just sat.

Mary's seatmate offered her a chunk of lamb skewered on her own knife, since she didn't seem to be feeding herself. Mary gripped the handle and risked another glance at Banquo.

He was gone as if he had not been there.

And of course, he hadn't been.

I, thought Mary, who lately met witches and heard prophecy and whose thumbs hurt so much I could cut them off with this knife, am now seeing ghosts. Saint Margaret and Saint Hilda, help me!

Her thumbs stopped pricking.

The relief was immense. She devoured her lamb.

When Macbeth returned, his Queen at his side, he was laughing out loud. "My worthy friends, forgive me." He strode easily, calmly, toward his seat, smiling at everyone. "Come, love and health to all. Give me some wine! Let's drink a toast!"

A boy rushed over with a cup, and another boy rushed to pour it full.

Bleeding Banquo held up his cup, too. He waved it back and forth in front of Macbeth, jeering in a manner most unlike friendly old Banquo.

Macbeth hurled his cup at Banquo. He had excellent aim. The wine-filled cup smashed into the tall back of the chair, spilled over the cushion, and spattered Lennox. "Get out, you horrible shadow!" bellowed Macbeth.

Banquo began to grin. His skeleton teeth grew larger and larger, until they were the teeth of horses.

The Queen was shaking. Not from watching Banquo – she didn't see him, either – but from the destruction of her feast. She was trying to think of a way to make this look normal. There was no way.

Macbeth shook his fist at his lords. "How can you look at such a sight and not turn pale?"

For a few moments, no one spoke. Then Lord Ross said, almost timidly, "What sight?"

The chair was empty.

Stand not upon the order of your going,
But go at once.
ACT III, SCENE 4

S WIN STOOD IN THE SERVICE HALL, A PLATTER ON HER SHOULDER. A footman took it and carried it into the dining hall. But the Queen of Scotland had given up the fight. She sagged and only with great effort summoned enough voice to speak. She dismissed the guests.

Swin watched them leave. Deer running from hounds could not have gone faster.

King Macbeth stood in the vast empty room, staring at his empty seat, as wide-eyed and frantic as any cornered stag. On the balcony, the musicians crept away. In the gallery, the jugglers melted in the shadows.

Swin went back to the kitchen and started in on the rice pudding.

There's but one down; the son is fled.
ACT III, SCENE 3

LEANCE SPENT THE NIGHT BLUNDERING THROUGH THICK WOODS.
When daylight came, he followed the flow of a stream. If
it emptied into the Tay, it would lead him past Scone.
Such a journey would take days, and he'd still have half Scotland
to cross. Fleance was shaking in his chest. It took him all night to
realize that it was rage coursing through him, heating his blood,
baking his brain.

He was furious with himself for not delivering fatal blows, not
saving his father. To think that the last thing his father said was
"Slave!" It hurt so much, stabbed so deep.

But with dawn's first light came the first flicker of understanding.

If those three killers had been plain old robbers, out for loot,
they would have wanted the valuable horses and the thick well-
made cloaks and sturdy leather boots worn by Fleance and his
father. They might have killed Banquo and Fleance, but they
would have done it afterward, so they didn't damage the goods.
And if they had been plain old robbers, one of them would not
have been wearing body armor – the mark of nobility.

If a man was already a lowlife, it was no insult to call him
slave. It was an insult only if the man was noble. Perhaps Banquo
had meant the attacker in armor. Fleance had not had the luxury

of time to gaze upon faces, being too occupied with weapons. What if Banquo had recognized his own killer?

Macbeth is a cur, his father had said. *He murdered Duncan with his own hands and hid his crime by slaughtering those innocent servants.*

What if, this time, Macbeth had not used his own hands? What if Macbeth had hired assassins?

To think Fleance had been honored by Macbeth's gentle benediction! How pretty had been the King's words — "May your horses be swift and sure of foot." But Macbeth had been laughing, because he had paid other men to be swift and sure of foot and to intercept Banquo and kill him. My father, thought Fleance, who loved Scotland with all his heart and mind and soul and body! Who bravely led the army of his honored king! King Duncan, that is.

Rage made Fleance not only swift and sure of foot but also careless of cold and hunger. He stormed on, because he had but one choice now: He must find the princes.

Fleance knew little about England. When a Scotsman went to England, he was desperate. The princes would have sought the protection of the English king, whose name Fleance vaguely thought was Edward. Kings did not like king killers. If Edward believed Prince Malcolm — that Macbeth achieved his throne by the murder of his predecessor — Edward would raise an army to help Prince Malcolm take back his rightful throne. And if Edward did not believe the prince, then Fleance, son of Banquo, must offer further proof.

Fleance thought briefly of Lady Mary. She had lost her father and the future she thought was secure, and he had pitied her.

Now he, too, had lost his father and the future he had thought was secure. Lady Mary, however, had to stay with Macbeth, who was a killer and who hired killers, and whose wife, according to Banquo, was a fiend herself. At least Fleance could avenge his father.

He came to a hovel of peat moss squares stacked like bricks. He called through the opening in the wall – not really a door – and asked for a place by the fire. They welcomed him, though they were afraid, because in remote places, the peasant must always fear the stranger. Fleance must not sleep here, though they offered a blanket; the murderers would slaughter this innocent family. When he was dry and warm, he said, "Tell no one about me," but their Gaelic was different from his own, and he was not sure they understood. Hospitality they did understand, and they gave him a stack of oatcakes and a staff of hazel wood. He felt balanced with the staff. It took away a little of the rage to stab the earth with its tough, hard tip. The cottager lit a fire candle for him, a rough splinter of pine, dripping with resin. It burned angrily, sizzling and flinging drops of hot sap in his face.

Fleance went on. He kept thinking of the prophecy. My father died because some old woman in a peat bog sang to Macbeth that *my* children will be kings? thought Fleance. My father died because Macbeth is afraid of my unborn children?

The two men in leather vests didn't matter to Fleance; they were hired hands. Only the third murderer mattered, the noble Macbeth had sent along to be sure that murder was done.

Who was the third murderer?

The stream was getting wider. Fleance was coming to its mouth, where it emptied into the sea or joined a larger river. A flat circular stone caught his eye. Its texture was warm and soothing, and it fit neatly in his palm.

Fleance picked up a rougher, harder stone and incised the flat stone with a single line across the middle. Then he gave the stone a quarter turn and incised a second line, to make a four-way cross. He held up the cross and swore an oath. "I will find the third murderer," Fleance promised his father. "And he will join Macbeth in hell."

Out, out, brief candle!
ACT V, SCENE 5

T HE FOLLOWING DAY DAWNED AS OVERCAST AND GLOOMY AS the day before and the day before that. At least it wasn't pouring.

The new king paced the battlements as if preparing for siege. Officers kept their distance.

Servants stayed in the shadows.

The crowds of yesterday were gone. The palace of Forres felt unused and dusty, like the chapel. Lady Mary slid into the Great Hall. No one had cleaned up. Noon? And the Queen had not yet examined the hall and seen this filth and chaos? She who had been fastidious – demanding – precise!

Mary walked slowly toward the dais. Slowly went up the two steps. Inch by inch approached Banquo's seat.

It was just a chair. Nothing on it. Nothing around it.

She chose not to turn her back to it. She worked her way out of the Great Hall, always facing the chair. She shut the two huge doors behind her, slid the well-oiled bolt, and just as smoothly, a piece of knowledge slid into her mind.

It was not just a chair.

It was the throne of Scotland.

And Macbeth, great Macbeth, had never sat in it.

. . . with a most indissoluble tie
For ever knit.
ACT III, SCENE 1

INVERNESS HAD HAD A KITCHEN GARDEN, WITH RICH SOIL AND HIGH walls to protect it from the endless north wind. But Forres had had a strolling garden with paths laid out in careful geometry and flowers to soften the edges. There were violets and roses and heliotrope. Fruit trees had been trained against the walls, their little branches sticking straight out at their sides. Rosemary and thyme and sweet rue scented the air.

The new queen tried to stroll. But leisure did not become her, or she could not find it. She stalked the diagonals and the circuits, neither sniffing the roses nor admiring the lilies.

Mary stayed close to Ildred, who stayed close to Lady Eglantyne. "Ildred, where is your darling little Dirle?" Eglantyne was asking.

Ildred shrugged. They were all doing that now – giving answers that weren't answers. Mary would not have believed that Ildred could shrug about Dirle.

"Lady Mary," called the Queen.

It was a relief to be addressed by her title. Mary hurried to the Queen's side. "You will soon be wed, Lady Mary," said the Queen.

The Queen, who knew everything, did not know about Asleif? "I believe my betrothed to have died," said Mary, avoiding the difficult fact that her betrothed had died fighting against Macbeth.

"Of course he died," said the Queen irritably. "And no loss, either. No. A gentleman has asked for your hand, and we have granted it."

A husband. He would take her away from here. She would not have to worry about murderers, or see ghosts, or fret over missing priests and dogs.

"Seyton has asked for your hand," said the Queen, "and you are his."

Seyton. So she was not given to some fat widower three times her age just because he wanted Shiel. Of course Seyton wanted Shiel, too, but he had a fine smile and once he had spoken kindly. Swin didn't like him. But Swin didn't know everything.

Seyton was Macbeth's man, though. He wouldn't leave this castle. Mary would never be allowed to leave the Macbeths at all.

Yet the choice of Seyton was puzzling. Why would a younger son of no particular worth be given such a prize as the lands of

Shiel? No one at court received rewards for nothing. Had Seyton fought so well on the sands that he had more right to Shiel than any other warrior? Or had Seyton done some special favor for Macbeth, which merited land and title?

She might find out, and she might not. She was just a girl through whom wealth passed. Soon she would enter that chapel on the second floor, holding a bouquet of these very flowers, and say to Seyton, "Sir, I become your wife." Then it would be done, done forever, and no undoing it.

To this announcement of a marriage, there was no round of applause from the ladies-in-waiting. No excited laughter. No congratulations.

Only Lady Ross spoke. Lady Ross — who knew no gloom. "Dear Lady Mary," she said, in her serene, warm voice, "we all so admire your courage in adversity and sorrow. But of course, my dear, you cannot be wed while you are in mourning." She said this with a peculiar emphasis, her eyes fixed on Mary. "Nor can you end your mourning early. To us, Lord Cawdor may have been a criminal and a traitor, but to you he was a loving father. It is right and just that you should mourn him. It will be some months before a wedding may properly take place."

Mary had no mourning clothes and lacked the courage to ask her lady to supply them. Certainly nobody else in Scotland was mourning the death of the traitor Cawdor. Today Mary wore an undershift of mustard yellow and an over-gown of buttercup yellow with white embroidery. Her braids fell fashionably down her cheeks, tied at the bottom with ribbons. Next to Lady Ross, she probably looked about ten years old.

Lady Ross swept the other ladies with her eyes. Her gaze landed hard on Eglantyne. "So beautifully said," agreed Eglantyne hastily. "However unworthy he is of tears, Lady Mary, however much Cawdor deserved his fate, you must spend time in mourning for your father."

Not one of these women had previously mentioned Mary's father to her.

"And that will give us time to plan the wedding," said Lady Ross, in her cheery spring-morning voice, "and to make a gown for Mary, won't it, dear highness? I think Mary looks best in green."

The Queen was not listening. She was staring at her dress with the horror Mary reserved for large spiders. The Queen flapped her hands, smacking the gown. "It smells of blood!" she shrieked.

"There's no blood, my queen," said Ildred, who had dealt with this before. "Your gown is clean."

But it was not her gown the Queen began washing. It was her hands. She washed them dry, in the air, while they stood in the garden among the roses.

Let every man be master of his time . . .
ACT III, SCENE 1

ILDRED WAS THE FIRST TO HEAR. "BANQUO," SHE SAID NUMBLY, STUMbling into the kitchen where Swin was about to deal with dinner. "Been murdered. They've found his body."

Ildred was shivering violently. It was catching. Swin began to feel like a fish at the end of a hook, twisting madly, as if she could still find the safety of the good clean water and the good swift swim.

Servants appeared like ants, girls from the buttery and pantry, men from the woodlot and the toolshed.

"Murdered on the heath," whispered Ildred. "Twenty wounds. Deep as trenches. From a battle-ax. They say any one slice of that ax would have killed him."

"Where'd they find him?" said Swin.

"In a ditch," said one of the men. "Think of it. King Duncan's commander – and they leave him lying in a muddy ditch like a dead sheep."

"Father and son rode off together," said Swin. "Was the boy killed, too?"

"The boy was not found. They say as how Banquo's son did the murder himself and now he's run."

Swin set down her own ax. She freed the hen she had meant to slaughter. She took off her canvas apron.

How could it happen twice – that a son murdered his father? How could it happen even once?

That old Aelgitha had said, *No one is sick. It's just time to leave.*

It's time, thought Swin.

Swin was not given to thoughts about loyalty. She didn't care about virtues that belonged to lords. She wasn't loyal to this king or that.

These people were cursed.

Swin was going home.

Two truths are told . . .

ACT I, SCENE 3

SEYTON RECEIVED PERMISSION FROM THE QUEEN TO WALK WITH Lady Mary. When he crooked his elbow and she put her little hand there, Seyton felt a thrill almost the equal of battle. He had what he wanted: He was admired by the king, and he was soon to be rich with castle and land.

She was small beside him, as a girl should be. Some of the women he had known – Ildred, for example – were big and rawboned. Some had been fighters. He liked that in a girl he forced down in the hay. Lady Mary had no fight to her, which was proper. Ladies weren't scullery maids.

Sure enough, Lady Mary spoke with longing to be saved by Seyton. "Let's go away," she pleaded. "Shiel is soft and good. It's far to the south. No murders happen there. We will find Father Ninian to wed us and . . . but we never found Father Ninian, did we?"

"Priests always look out for themselves," said Seyton with a shrug. "And there's always another priest somewhere. Sweet Mary, Lady Ross persuaded the Queen you need months of mourning. That's nonsense. We need to undo what Lady Ross said. If you speak to the Queen, she'd change her mind." He gave her his best smile. "A swift wedding means a joyous life."

She looked up at him. Her green eyes were huge and lovely, her lips a pink rosebud. "Good sir," she said, trembling.

To be called "sir" by a lady – wonderful. And to know that his mere presence made her tremble – wonderful.

In her shivery, uncertain voice, Lady Mary said, 'Do you believe, sir, that Fleance killed his own father?'

Seyton was glad to get this straight. 'Fleance? He's a worm. He couldn't kill a rabbit, never mind a man. Soon they'll catch Banquo's murderers. I have an idea where to find them.'

Lady Mary frowned slightly. It was adorable, that little crease between her eyes as she tried to think. 'Didn't Fleance kill a heavily armed soldier on the beach?' she asked.

Seyton laughed. 'Fleance couldn't even hang on to his sword. I killed that one for him. A nice solid stab through the back. Might as well dishonor them, those traitors.'

* * *

. . . the vile blows and buffets of the world . . .
ACT III, SCENE 1

* * *

THE DAYS CREPT BY.

The ladies-in-waiting laughed and sang and stitched at the embroidery of a battle scene that had not happened exactly as the Queen sketched it. Each new companion left early and soon. All but Lady Ross seemed to have ailing mothers or doddering old fathers-in-law to nurse. And now it was Eglantyne leaving in the carriage her husband's men had brought.

"Dear Ildred," said Eglantyne, kissing her good-bye, "you must be brave."

When they were little girls, Ildred had not known how different her life would be from Eglantyne's. "Take me with you, Egga. Please."

"I cannot take you. It is dangerous even for me to leave so soon."

"You are with child, Egga," Ildred reminded her. "Of course you must go home, you cannot be riding horses or lifting. Tell the Queen you need me to help you."

"You have been my true friend," said Eglantyne. "You thought of pretending that I'm going to have a baby. You told everyone I was sick in the morning. You're the reason the Queen believes the story. But bringing you with me would be carrying it too far, Illy. Even the Queen, distracted as she is, would have some questions."

"No, Egga, she wouldn't. She's too upset. You be the one to ask Lady Macbeth to let me go with you."

Eglantyne pretended Ildred was not begging to go along. "No one wants to call her queen, do they?" said Eglantyne.

Ildred lowered her voice. Barely moving her lips, she breathed, "I'm afraid."

"We're all afraid. Gracious Duncan, dead in the very bedroom of Macbeth? Gracious Malcolm and Donalbain, killers of their father? But they fled, didn't they? How it did grieve our lord Macbeth. How his heart hurt. Of course he slew the two servants! Who wouldn't have?" Eglantyne crossed herself. "A man who wanted the truth wouldn't have. And now we are to believe that Banquo is dead by the hand of Fleance, who never did anything in his life except shadow his father?"

Ildred wet her lips. "Egga, help me."

"I can't. You have to cover for me. That way I can slip away. But if you disappeared, *you* she would notice. You're her servant."

Eglantyne could not have said anything more painful.

"They won't hurt you," said Eglantyne, getting into the carriage. "They hurt only ones with power." She closed the draperies in Ildred's face. The carriage left.

"You're wrong," whispered Ildred. "They hurt anyone in their path."

Once more she stood in the rain. Troops of friends?

Sweet Jesus, she prayed, *send me even one friend.*

⁓

O, never
Shall sun that morrow see!
ACT I, SCENE 5

⁓

EYTON SAUNTERED IN AND BOWED WITH GREAT DRAMA. "YOUR highness. Ladies. My dear queen, may I escort you to the hanging?"

Mary could not abide the sight of him. Why hadn't she realized that her thumbs pricked when she was in the presence of *Seyton* — not when she was with Fleance? Now two murderers had betrothed her to a third murderer, while Fleance, who had been kind to Mary, and Prince Malcolm, who had been kind to Ildred, were on the run.

Seyton winked at Mary. Mary studied her embroidery. The

Queen stared dully at Seyton. "Hanging?" she said. Her voice was blurred.

Seyton offered his arm. "I am told that you are sleeping poorly, your highness. It'll do you good to see Lord Banquo's murderers hanged. Once they're dead, it'll all stop. This pall over your blessed reign will come to an end."

"Come to an end?" The Queen sounded like a child hardly daring to hope.

Mary loved her again. She cannot have known what was happening, Mary told herself. She is as shocked to be married to a murderer as I am to wed one.

Seyton had told Mary he might know where Banquo's murderers were. Sure enough, he had found them. Yet how could he have known who they were? And how could he have found them so easily? Two strangers in the night on a faraway heath?

The Queen took Seyton's arm. "You are sure that these are the murderers of Banquo?" Her voice quavered.

"I interrogated them myself," he told her.

With this man, Mary of Shiel would spend her life. What had Lady Ross known about him, that she had forced the postponement of Mary's wedding? What had Swin known, long ago in the kitchen at Inverness, when she raised her chopping blade in Seyton's face?

Swin, who had vanished. *Saint Hilda,* Mary prayed. *Guide and direct Swin in all she does. Keep her safe. Let her be forgotten by those who love to hurt.*

Seyton and the Queen left the solar.

"I heard a rumor that there were three murderers," said Ildred. "Yet only two are being hanged."

"They say these two were hired," said Lady Ross, taking out the Queen's uneven stitches and doing them over properly. "They say the third murderer is still out there. They should have forced the two men they caught to tell who the third murderer is."

"They cannot be forced to talk," said Ildred. "Seyton cut out their tongues when he was torturing them."

God's benison go with you and with those
That would make good of bad, and friends of foes!
ACT II, SCENE 4

THE LADIES SAT IN THE SOLAR AS IF IN PRISON, GRIMLY SEWING.
Watching the hangings had not brought peace to Lady Macbeth. Today she could not thread her needle. She would lick the little stub and flatten it between her fingers. But her hands were trembling, and she could not get the silk through the eye. This time she stabbed her palm and drew blood. "Now, now," said Lady Ross. "Let's bathe that poor hand." She snapped her fingers for a basin of water, and, when it came, set it next to the Queen. The Queen plunged both hands in the water and began scrubbing as if the single drop of blood from the sharp needle had been a pint.

Ildred heard a dog bark.

The Queen continued to scrub her hands.

Ildred stood up. Set down her mending. Curtsied to the unseeing Queen.

Lady Ross caught the Queen's thin white fingers in her own and massaged lanolin into them, crooning, "All the bad news is over now."

Ildred left the solar. Shut the door. Raced down the stairs. Rushed into the forecourt and out the gate.

Dirle was hurrying just as fast to reach her. He met her midair, barking and whining and yipping with joy. She hugged him, and he wriggled down and spun around and leaped back up to lick her face, dashed in circles, and leaped into her arms again.

Sweet Jesus *had* given her one friend, and that one friend was, after all, the most loyal of all. "Hello, my daughter," said Father Ninian. "I'm glad to see you glad."

Dirle's tail was whapping so hard and fast it was going to bruise her. The palace guards had dogs of their own and smiled to see this dog-joy. They lowered their lances and leaned on the shafts.

"What took you so long, Father?" cried Ildred.

"Oh, my daughter, so many things to attend to. You knew I had to take care of the poor old grandfather of Swin. What was he to do without her? She couldn't coax him to leave his old hut, where he lived all his life. He is blind, you know, but he loves his little glen and the birds singing in the trees and his old collie at his side. If he had come to the castle, Swin could have tucked him in some corner and fed him scraps, but he wouldn't. I wouldn't, either, in his place. Then after I dealt with the grandfather, there were the widows, of course, and the children. You were wonderful to let me keep Dirle by my side. I felt much safer walking in those woods with a dog. In these perilous times, it's good to have a friend who barks."

Ildred wondered if the priest had known that Swin stole all the food she gave to her grandfather. Of course he knew, she thought. And probably gave the grandfather more. "What widows?" she said.

Father Ninian took her arm as if on a stroll through a garden, but the route he took led down the hill and away from Forres. Dirle darted between and around them, tail wagging, bark never stopping. It was not a stealthy departure.

"Widows of the two servants knifed by Macbeth. Their poor wives had nothing. And the second set of widows who are my burden now – their husbands did, in fact, kill Banquo. The wives said they were desperate men gone bad and would do anything for money. Do you know, my dear Ildred, there is no man on earth so low that some woman – some mother, wife, or daughter – doesn't love him? Those men Seyton just hanged were loved. And if they were paid to do that murder, the money didn't find its way to their wives. Between them, they have nine mouths to feed."

"I was the ninth child in my family," said Ildred.

"I remember." Father Ninian walked swiftly for a man of his age. They were almost in the trees. Every castle Ildred had ever seen was on a bare hill, with bare land around and trees beyond.

"I have had a thought, Ildred." Father Ninian opened his hand. Lying in his palm was a spectacular diamond. His twinkling eyes matched the twinkle of the gem. "I found this in the poultry pen when I was catching a nice fat hen for Swin's grandfather. I think perhaps a goose ate it, and it came out the other end. I did have to wash it off."

The diamond had rolled out the back door of the kitchen into the poultry yard? So Swin had been wrong about dead-lights. On the other hand, that was a long way to roll. Perhaps some bright angel had wanted the diamond for Father Ninian.

They had walked quite a distance in a short time. They were into the trees now, and there, tied to a branch, nibbling at ground cover, were two ponies. One had a bright-red leather sidesaddle, with the center pommel for holding tight and the side pommel for hooking the knee. Father Ninian handed Ildred the reins of the pony with the sidesaddle. "My bishop thinks that with this diamond I can rebuild a little church I've always had my eye on. A caved-in chapel, far out on the moor."

"Out on that blasted heath?" demanded Ildred. "I know the chapel you mean. They say witches camp there."

Father Ninian laughed.

"You're a parish priest," she protested. "Are you going to become a monk who lives alone and prays alone and stays away from man?"

"No, no. I haven't the temperament for that. I love my fellow man. Well, most of them. I fear Macbeth has chosen Satan. Power is such a great temptation. Satan thought power would tempt even our Lord Jesus Christ. He was one of the few who withstood the temptation of power, I think. No, Ildred, my dear, on the moor live the desperately poor, the deformed, and the lepers. They need me." He mounted his pony, and she mounted hers. He clucked his tongue at Dirle. The dog gathered himself and leaped, not quite high enough, so Father Ninian bent over to haul him up.

"I need a housekeeper," said Father Ninian, nudging the pony into the forest. "And I thought perhaps you would take to your bosom the youngest of those nine children. A baby girl. Not six months old. The mother doesn't want it. Or rather, she wants it but cannot feed it."

Father Ninian was a fine rider. He and his pony shot forward into the woods. Ildred caught up and rode very close so Dirle could step onto her lap instead. "Are we in a hurry?" she asked, kissing and fondling her dog.

"Along with all who seek to leave the King's side," said the priest. "We melt into the forest and vanish on the moor, as did our friend Swin, and perhaps the day will come when we emerge, and perhaps it will not. Ildred, you know what it is to be unwanted. And you are full of love. No one could be a better mother than you. I believe you prayed to have a friend. The prayer was thoroughly answered. You have a dog and a daughter as well."

Ildred looked back. Forres was not visible through the thick green leaves. She shivered once for Lady Mary, but she could not rescue Mary, nor end her betrothal to Seyton.

Mary of Shiel was on her own.

CHAPTER 11

O, full of scorpions is my mind, dear wife!
ACT III, SCENE 2

IN THE SOLAR, THEIR HANDS VERY CLEAN FROM CALMING THE QUEEN, their throats soft and comforted after drinking the hot posset Mary had brought, the Queen, Lady Ross, and Mary listened to an uproar in the courtyard.

Mary was brushing the Queen's hair, a task inherited from Ildred. The troops of friends were disappearing in the glens, rowing down the rivers, finding distant family. The Queen did not ask after them, although sometimes she stared at the seat where a friend had lately sat.

Mary's mother had died young, and yet, while she lived, had a world full of joy. Lady Macbeth lived in a world without joy. Every day the ranks were thinner, the laughter dimmer.

Rents were coming in. Many men worked off their rent with unpaid labor. They would tend the kennels, shear sheep, dig new latrines, repair stone walls. Other men came in with rent in kind: grain, hay, honey, wool, dried fish, firewood.

No one stayed.

Some even claimed they dared not enter the castle gate but had to negotiate their business outside the walls.

Mary found scraps of happiness. Along the river she watched otters play. She embroidered in gold and turned her work to see it glisten in the sun. She fed the chickens and geese herself, because there was something so companionable about the way they bobbed around her feet, clucking and honking, and because they reminded her of Swin, who did what she needed to do. What do I need to do? wondered Mary.

"Lovely!" cried Lady Ross, holding up the hand mirror. "Wait until our king your dear husband sees you! He will be so delighted."

This was unlikely. Macbeth no longer noticed the wife he had loved so well. He did not visit Lady Macbeth much, nor did she go to him.

Mary thought of her as Lady Macbeth again and not as the Queen. The title did not sit well on those shaky shoulders. But what could – built on a foundation of murder?

The ruckus in the courtyard could no longer be ignored.

"It's not enough that *Malcolm* has gone to King Edward to raise an army against me?" screamed the King. "It's not enough that

that stupid little whey-faced son of Banquo joined him? Now *Macduff* has gone to Edward?"

The Queen jumped to her feet, flinging her embroidery canvas against the wall and slamming her half-finished posset to the floor. "Macduff!" she sobbed. "No! I won't believe that! He loves my lord Macbeth! *We are friends!*" Lady Macbeth staggered to the stairs, and Lady Ross followed. Mary tagged along. She had become part of the furniture and, like a servant, was noticed only in her absence.

The Queen advanced into the courtyard. Lady Ross and Mary stayed in the shadows, unwilling to draw the King's rage.

"I won't accept it!" bellowed the King. "Macduff swore to me!"

"They say," the messenger went on nervously, "that King Edward will bring his general Siward out of retirement to fight. They say King Edward is to champion the cause of Prince Malcolm."

The King noticed his wife. Mary was so glad when Macbeth held out his hand to her and so glad to see the Queen kiss her husband's hand. There was something dreadful about their aloneness. They had gotten the world and at what price? Without friends, what worth does the world have?

"We face war," said the King to his queen, and for a moment Mary thought they would comfort each other. But Macbeth turned away, calling for his advisers, and the Queen stood alone.

. . . does he feel
His secret murders sticking on his hands.
ACT V, SCENE 2

MALCOLM WAS NO LONGER THE SLEEK, GLAMOROUS YOUNG prince Fleance had so admired at the feast. Malcolm was worn out by a battle that had not yet begun. "So Macbeth killed your father, too, Fleance." The prince held his head in his hands as if it could not fit more bad news. "Scotland, my Scotland. How she bleeds. Tell me how your dear father Banquo died."

"He died saving me. Two kerns and a noble attacked us in the night as we fled to you."

"Was there time to fight back?" asked Malcolm.

"We were not sensible enough to arm ourselves for attack," said Fleance, and now this struck him as astonishing. His father had been explaining how Macbeth planned to murder them both, explaining they had to run so they would not be murdered! And yet neither father nor son bothered to arm. Thoughts of the Weird Ones filled him. Had they caused Fleance and Banquo to be unready?

"We thought we were riding safely ahead of Macbeth," Fleance told the prince. "We were wrong. Bare hands are not weapons against three men with battle-axes. I wounded one with my knife and slashed another, and then my father was dying and I was running."

"You are fortunate," said the prince sadly. "I ran without trying to avenge my father. I put my own safety first." He stared mournfully out a window at English trees on English soil. "I didn't expect to be king so soon. That's my excuse for behavior less than royal," said Malcolm as if Fleance had accused him of something.

Fleance tried to rally the prince. "But you are alive and have time to become the royal leader you were born to be. I know that you will triumph. We thought the world was good and the future was soft, my prince, but we were wrong. My father realized that each new morning, Macbeth would make new widows and new orphans. But in the face of all evidence, I was as a child. I saw nothing. I didn't believe my father until he was dead."

"I'm still a child," agreed Malcolm. "A virgin in all ways – to women, to the battlefield, and to the world."

"You fought on the beach against Norway, though."

"Not really. My father had my brother and me deeply protected. We just played war on the edges. Who knew that it was our father who needed the protection? I thought Lord and Lady Macbeth were wonderful. I was so proud of my father and so sorry for that little Lady Mary. I hear she's been affianced to Macbeth's lackey, Seyton."

Lady Mary would wed Seyton? Fleance had pain in his chest.

"But there is good news," said Malcolm. "King Edward has assigned his finest general, Siward, to me and loaned me ten thousand troops to bring against Macbeth. Siward's army has already begun to move north. Every day we delay reaching Scotland, new sorrows strike heaven in the face."

And so Fleance had scarcely scraped the mud from his boots when he joined an army marching back north. With every step, he pondered Malcolm's remark. How could heaven be struck by anything, let alone sorrow?

But it was heaven most badly hurt by the cruelty of man — heaven, where they hoped that good would triumph. Heaven, where angels are bright still, though the brightest fell.

Fleance was thinking of Satan, a bright angel who had fallen to hell, and of Duncan, God's bright king on earth, felled by Macbeth. Then he dreamed of Mary, a bright star thrown aside by her father and fallen to a dark future.

He had a sudden eerie sense of being next to Mary, so close that everything happening to Mary was happening to him. Sweating horse and burning wood, jagged lightning and cruel fire. Fleance gasped for air because her lungs ran out of air, was weak because her heartbeat slowed, stumbled because her feet sank in the mire.

He remembered now that the serving girls and the stable hands pronounced Seyton's name in the old Scots way.

Satan.

Curses not loud but deep . . .
ACT V, SCENE 3

MACBETH COULD NOT STAY AT FORRES, FAR IN THE NORTH ON the shore. If he did, the English army would have to cross two-thirds of Scotland to fight him, and this would put Scotland in another kind of danger: The English king would be very tempted to keep that two-thirds for England. It was an unthinkable risk. Macbeth must march as close to England as his strongest castle and fight from there.

Dunsinane was the word on every lip now.

Dun was the old word for castle. Old words always made Mary think of the estate Asleif would never give her, and the glad stone on which she would never stand.

Once again, the axles creaked and the wooden wheels groaned as the court of King Macbeth moved to Dunsinane.

They passed a roadside cross. We did not have a mass of the dead for Lord Banquo, thought Mary. How could the King pretend to mourn Banquo as his lost friend and not celebrate his life?

The rain came down. People tugged hoods over their heads and faces like masked robbers. Warm and invisible in her cloak, Mary found herself riding alongside Seyton and the King. Slung over the pommel of her saddle was a small leather bag, which had once belonged to a son of Duncan. It was filled with the clothing and weapons of that son of Duncan. But Macbeth, perhaps the son of a devil, did not see Mary, let alone her baggage, and the eyes and ears of Seyton were fixed on his king.

Seyton, killer of Asleif. Who had won Mary's hand for doing some unknown deed. Who cut out the tongues of men for the fun of it, since they would be hanged anyway . . . or to stop them from talking.

The King said one word to Seyton. One word, without instruction. "Macduff," spat Macbeth, and then the King whipped his horse and galloped ahead, as if to distance himself from what he had said.

But what was wrong with uttering the name of his friend Macduff?

Mary kept her head low and nudged her pony to the far side of a cart. A row of carts passed by while she waited. Through gaps, she saw Seyton signal his groom.

Mary's thumbs pricked. She lifted her thumbs to her eyes, to see what was happening to her poor hands, and it made her eyes prick as well, like brambles in the brain.

If Seyton should notice her, Mary planned to rush to his side and give him an adoring smile. She would cry proudly, "I saw you speaking to our good Macbeth. Did the King give you a commission?" She would squeeze his hand. "Am I to be made even more proud of my warrior?"

But Seyton did not see her. Like Macbeth, he had forgotten women. He had larger things to do. And those things he and the King had to do – were they evil things?

Once more the royal train came to a stone marking the intersection of roads. Not a cross this time, but an ancient shaft carved with tall, thin warriors carrying tall, thin shields.

The procession continued on its slow and dreary path south.

Seyton kicked his big, beautiful chestnut. The stallion was excited and eager to run and didn't care about wind and rain. East the horse flew, bearing his rider away from the wagon train.

Mary was puzzled. Macduff had gone to England. England was south. There was nothing in the east.

Except Macduff's castle, Falkland. That was east. Macduff's home in Fife, where his little chicks played.

Mary was cold then, with a chill no fleece could prevent. Falkland. Where Macduff's chicks played.

Mary caught up to Seyton's groom. She squared her shoulders. She was the future wife of this man's master. She would one day rule this man's world. She spoke in the voice that required a full answer. "Will my lord Seyton reach Falkland by nightfall?"

"Not by nightfall, my lady. And the weather being so bad for so long, the burns overflowing, the peat soggy and dangerous – it'll be a longer ride to Fife than usual. But don't you worry. Nothing out there can hurt him, where he's going."

No. Wife and chicks couldn't hurt Seyton. And that was why Seyton hadn't picked up armor or lances, battle-ax or claymore. Any knife would do. He could enter Falkland castle as a friend and saunter out as a murderer.

Mary let the groom go.

Officers rode on. Pack animals responded to whips on their backs. Men and women trudged, enduring wind and weather, hoping the fire at Dunsinane would be blazing and the soup hot.

Lady Mary of Shiel rode out onto the blasted heath to stop Seyton.

The Weird Sisters, hand in hand,
Posters of the sea and land,
Thus do go about, about . . .
ACT I, SCENE 3

SEYTON WAS LOST.

He was furious at himself, furious at the moor and the wind and the weather.

Every saddle of land, soft with grass, but difficult of footing because of hummocks and puddles, looked exactly like the last one. There was no sun to guide him. Over the low-lying land, mist gathered in puffy folds, tangled like piles of shorn wool, tumbling down on Seyton and trying to suffocate him.

Twice now he had passed the same tower. At first he thought it was a stone escape turret built by the ancients. Scotland was dotted with these, because hiding places from invaders had been necessary from time immemorial. Now he rode up to it. It was not made by man. It was a huge oak, jaggedly broken off about twenty feet up. Lightning had struck, burning a trail along the trunk and knocking off the top of the tree. Seyton peered through a small cleft at the ground and found that the vast trunk was hollow. If a person could fit through the hole, he could live there.

A moment of sun gave Seyton his bearings. He flicked the reins and headed east. He had gone a mile, perhaps two, when distantly, faintly, he heard his name called.

His skin prickled. Was he to meet the Weird Ones here? He had met them once and brought the gift they required. Even for Seyton it had taken guts to do it. He felt sick sometimes, remembering it.

He owed the Weird Ones. They had made him first with the new king. They had given him Lady Mary's hand. It was not pleasant to owe witches a favor. But this heath was a hundred miles away from those Weird Ones. Perhaps miles didn't matter to them. Or maybe other witches owned this heath.

He could not ignore them now.

Seyton reined in and looked for the witches.

There was only one, and she on horseback.

"Seyton!" called the rider. "Seyton!"

He could not believe his eyes. It was Lady Mary.

The multiplying villainies of nature
Do swarm upon him . . .
ACT I, SCENE 2

I FOLLOWED YOU!" MARY CRIED GAILY, SO HE WOULD THINK THAT HER journey had been a joy and a privilege. Then she pouted. "You didn't even pause to say good-bye to me. I thought we were becoming close."

Clearly, he had no idea what to do with her. And just as clearly, he was touched and thrilled that she had followed him. Mary tried to use this. "My place is beside you," she pleaded.

He regarded her uncertainly. Mary dismounted, to make it harder for him to continue east. "Oh, Seyton, so many have abandoned the King. I was so afraid you were abandoning him and me both. We have such a future ahead of us. No one will have seen that we ran. Come. Let's go back and catch up with the wagon train."

She had made an error, accusing him of running.

"I would never run. Never. I have a commission from the King. You should not have left the baggage train. The moor is dangerous. Your place is beside our queen."

I am to be married to him anyway, thought Mary. I have seen what married people do. Well, actually I haven't. But I have seen what horses do. Perhaps that will keep Seyton from riding on.

Mary stroked Seyton's thigh.

But riding so hard, so fast, had left her windblown. Her cloak and gown were in disarray.

"You're carrying a dagger?" said Seyton.

Her hand flew to the knife of Malcolm or Donalbain. She thought quickly. "Only a fool goes unarmed," she pointed out.

Seyton laughed. "I would not have thought you would even dare hold a knife. But I have a commission to carry out, and I cannot take you with me. Return to the baggage train." Seyton reached down and plucked Mary's dirk from its place at her waist.

"I don't want to ride back alone," she pleaded. "The moor is frightening. I'm scared. Please come back with me."

Seyton sighed. "Mount up," he said.

But when she was astride her little pony, he took Mary's reins from her hands. It left her powerless. "We're going back?" she cried. "Oh, sir, thank you! You are so kind."

"I'm not going back. I have to put you somewhere until I'm done, and I know just the place. I shouldn't be so surprised. The Weird Ones must have led me there. Not once, but twice, so I'd remember."

"What do you mean – until you're done?" said Mary. "Done doing what?"

"It is best for you not to know."

They rode on in silence. A strange towerlike place appeared. If ever there was a place where the Weird Ones lived, this was it. A bent, slick, un-stone tower contrived of some witchly material –

No. It was a hollow tree, blasted by lightning, its center burned out.

Like Lady Macbeth, thought Mary.

"You'll be safe in here," said Seyton. "You're going to crawl through that tiny opening, I'm going to wedge this fallen limb in the hole so nothing can get in there with you, and you're going to sit here quietly until I come back. It won't be long."

If Mary was shut up in there, she could not save Lady Macduff. Flirting and pouting had not achieved Mary's ends. Perhaps lying would. "I know you're going to arrest Lady Macduff. The Queen was talking about it. I understand the King's rage. Of course he loved Lord Macduff, and he feels betrayed, and he has been betrayed! But –"

Seyton twisted her arm behind her back and yanked the bones viciously upward. "You didn't come for love, then?"

He would gladly break her arm. Mary tried to save herself. "Of course I love you. What else would give me the courage to be alone on the moor except knowing that soon I would be with you? But when you tell Lady Macduff what her husband has done, there should be a woman to attend her. I can help. You will be glad to have me."

Seyton regarded her silently. She had almost convinced him. "Lady Macbeth loves Lady Macduff," Mary lied. "The Queen wants dear Lady Macduff to be all right. She suggested I should come after you. To care for their little chicks."

"Really?" said Seyton. "That's interesting. I would not have said the Queen cared about other people's children. She once said to me that she would dash her own baby's head against a wall if that was what it took to get power."

"She did not!" cried Mary. "That's a terrible thing to say!"

"She's a terrible woman," said Seyton. He seized Mary like a sack of barley and began shoveling her into the hole. Mary fought back, and he started to grin. He liked struggle. The struggle began to take on another aspect. It was better to be where Seyton could not touch her. Mary slithered inside the tree, beyond his reach.

The inner sides were slick and black, like some awful pot on some awful stove. There were no protrusions she could hang on to or climb up. The jagged, ugly top of the oak was many feet above her head.

"Will you give my love to Lady Macduff?" Mary quavered.

Seyton's voice was farther away. "I'm not sending her love. I'm not taking her prisoner."

The owl wins against the wren.

In the witches' song, I am not the wren, thought Mary. Lady Macduff is. Nor is Macbeth the owl – Seyton is.

What do owls do to wrens?

Tear them to pieces.

CHAPTER 12

. . . there shall be done a deed of dreadful note.

ACT III, SCENE 2

THE HEAVENS SPLIT OPEN IN A STORM SO BRUTAL THAT MARY WAS bruised by the rain.

The wind screamed through a knothole in the vast trunk.

No wonder the sides were slick as glass, if for decades they had been worn down by winds like this. She wept. In this world of evil, it was hard to find that glad stone on which to stand. "Saint Hilda!" she shouted over the din of the storm. "Saint Margaret! Save me! Let me out!"

Lightning struck.

The tree was used to this. Mary was not. Thunder crashed in her ears. Fire leaped up in her face. Smoke filled her lungs.

~

How did you dare
To trade and traffic with Macbeth
In riddles and affairs of death . . .
ACT III, SCENE 5

~

S EYTON'S HORSE WAS NERVOUS OF ITS FOOTING ACROSS ALL THE rock and cleft and stone. It was a relief to reach a smooth green meadow. But the chestnut stallion would not cross it. Seyton kicked hard, but the horse shied and tried to disobey.

Seyton was sick of disobedience. Who would have guessed that stupid little Lady Mary would dare charge after him? And then to lie! To pretend love – even pretend weakness! When all along, she had armed herself with a dirk. She had hurt him. How dare she? She would pay.

Seyton whipped his horse.

It tried to throw him.

He hadn't let Mary throw him off, and he wasn't letting some stupid horse do it. He kicked and whipped and hauled on the reins and, finally, forward into the green grass the stallion ran, and the soft earth became a bog, and the horse sank.

Seyton screamed to the Weird Ones for help before he realized they were the force dragging his horse down. "I'll give it to you!" he shouted. "Whatever you want! What do you want?"

But if they answered, the screams and grunts of his horse drowned them out.

The horse was already sunk to its knees, thrashing harder, sinking faster.

If I don't let my hands or feet puncture the surface of the swamp, if I keep myself long and spread out and weightless, keep rolling and moving, I can get out of here.

Seyton almost prayed. Then he laughed. He had stepped too far away from prayer to use it now.

Wisdom? To leave his wife, to leave his babes . . .
ACT IV, SCENE 2

MARY EXPECTED TO BE BURNED TO CINDERS, BUT WHEN THE fire ended, the only sign that lightning had struck was another slash in the tree. The tiny slot through which Seyton had forced Mary now went all the way up the great trunk. Mary stepped out onto the moor and was free. Her pony trotted over, as if it had been waiting all this time. She slid out of her gown, filthy now with mud, rain, and smoke. From her pack, still hanging by the saddle, she took the prince's trousers, tunic, cape, and cap, and then stuffed her gown into the bag.

She was exhausted from fear, cold, and hunger. She rubbed her eyes, and her hand came away black. She was sooty from the lightning fire. But that was good; it was a disguise.

It was possible that Seyton's stallion – a magnificent charger in battle – would be terrified by this lightning storm. Seyton might have to seek shelter until the storm passed by. But Mary rode a Highland pony, which knew by instinct where to put its fat little hoofs. She nestled down into its tangled mane and whispered, "Go like the wind!" They hurtled through the mist, came out into daylight, and found the road. Not one hoofprint marked the mud ahead of them.

Seyton was behind her!

Seyton did not plan to arrest Lady Macduff. So what was he going to do? Surely he would not kill her, thought Mary. She is an innocent. I wasn't killed when my father turned traitor on his king. They cannot execute Lady Macduff just because her husband turned traitor on this king.

And then ahead she saw Falkland, a very different castle from any Mary had ever occupied. There was a tower into which the occupants could bolt when they were threatened, and whose doors they could seal, but all the living spaces were open to the world. There was not even an enclosed courtyard! Never mind gates and battlements, parapets and moats. Two huge stone buildings stood at angles to each other, making a sheltered ell for gardens and horses and, above all, children.

The children were scampering over the grass, which was strewn with toys and balls and fishing rods. Pet geese wore ribbons and puppies tripped over one another. The children rushed to greet her.

"We just had another visitor!" cried one.

"Are you a boy or a girl?" asked another, eyeing Mary uncertainly.

"You need a bath," said a third one.

"But stay," said the first. "Our other visitor, Uncle Ross, he wouldn't stay."

"Lord Ross was here?" said Mary. How many people were rushing over the heath, racing through storms, trying to reach Falkland first?

"Lord Ross explained how our father went to join the King of England," said the oldest child proudly.

"Which is not a good thing," said the tiniest. "He should be here keeping us safe."

"Papa isn't a traitor, is he?" demanded the middle child, anxiously.

"No," said Lady Macduff, striding out of the castle – although by Mary's definition it was no castle, just a very large stone house. What had Lord Macduff been thinking, to leave his chicks at a defenseless place like this?

"Cawdor was the traitor, not my husband. And who are you?" said Lady Macduff, frowning at Mary, as well she might – a filthy, mud-spattered, horse-stinking boy in clothes far too big.

"I am not known to you," said Mary, although this was not true. Lady Macduff had known her father, Cawdor, well. If Mary admitted that she was his daughter, Lady Macduff wouldn't listen to a word she said. So Mary skipped that part of the story. "I am merely a messenger. I have come to warn you of danger. The world is against you, as it is against all who are gentle and good."

"So I've heard," said Lady Macduff irritably. "My brother told me that my husband, who *ought* to be here at my side, took it into his head to go to *England*. Even the wren stays at the nest to defend her babies from the owl! But did *my* husband stay? No. Did he think of *us*? No. Does he *love* us? No."

He does love you, thought Mary. He talks so often of his wife and chicks. "Lady Macduff, since the owl *does* win against the wren, you must leave. It is known that you are here. Go to another of your castles. This is unsafe. Or get into that tower, and bolt it, and let *no man* into your home."

"No. This is my home, and here we stay. This ugliness abroad in Scotland will cease eventually. I do not run. Running is for cowards."

"You must run! Evil comes upon you."

"I have done no harm," snapped Lady Macduff. "But I remember now, I am in this earthly world, where to do harm is laudable folly and to do good is sometimes dangerous. But I refuse to be afraid, and I refuse to run."

"Your tower is part of your home," pleaded Mary. "Lock yourselves in there."

"No. My home is open to friends and neighbors."

"But it is also open to your foes! Macbeth is killing people who oppose him."

"I do not oppose him. I have no foes. I am not involved in politics. I do not care who is king. I have no opinions on anything except how to rear my children."

"They will hurt you," shouted Mary, "because they cannot hurt Macduff himself."

"Nonsense. Now you look terrified. If you're going to run, boy, run. Here, take some oatcakes for your journey."

The oatcakes were on a plate, probably meant for the children to share. They were beautiful children, full of talk and light. Mary ached to stay. What a pleasure their chatter would be after the terrible months with the Queen.

Mary offered the plate to the children, but they shook their heads, so she stuffed the oatcakes into Malcolm's bag and climbed back on her pony. Far down the road she spied somebody striding on foot toward Falkland.

Seyton would be on his stallion. A peasant walking on a path was no worry. "Fly," she begged Lady Macduff.

"Let others run," said the lady.

Thou art the best of the cut-throats!
ACT III, SCENE 4

SEYTON'S HANDS WERE DAMP AND COLD. HE KEPT WIPING THEM ON his riding trousers, unable to forget what he had done with those hands; unable to clean them; unable to get rid of the scarlet sticky dripping of blood.

He walked faster, pounded harder, went up hill and down, but he remained chilled.

He wondered vaguely if there had been enough heat and sun this summer for a good harvest or if there was to be famine in the land. It was a terrible beginning for the reign of King Macbeth.

Going back across that green boggy land was a nightmare. Every time he put a foot down he wondered how far it would sink. Sometimes he threw rocks at the grass, testing. His magnificent chestnut – not his, really, but Macbeth's – was gone forever, or so he assumed. He hadn't looked back to see if the horse got out of the mire.

Walking, as if he were some kern, made him furious. His own terror made him even more angry. Once he got back to that hollow tree he would ride Mary's pony. Let her walk. She deserved it.

Seyton spent a sleepless night on a high rock, using his boots for a pillow. Every time he closed his eyes, he saw the eyes of Lady Macduff at that terrible moment when she realized what was going to happen. But if he didn't close his eyes and stared up at the starry night, her soul drifted above, watching him.

In the morning, Seyton trudged on. Around noon, he found the hollow tree right where he had left it. Had he expected it to move? Had he thought the Weird Ones could take their tree with them?

Lady Mary was still sitting inside the hollow, but it was a different tree from the one he had left, and she was a different girl. The tree itself had been riven in half. Mary was covered with soot and mud. "Lightning?" he asked, walking right in.

Mary did not speak. She looked stunned, as if the lightning had hit her, too. That happened sometimes; people didn't always recover their wits. Well, if she turned out to be a fool, he would still get her land and title.

Her little shaggy pony shied away every time Seyton got close. He forced Mary to catch her own pony. The pony wasn't big enough to carry both of them. Their pace was slow. The girl couldn't, or wouldn't, pick up her feet.

They came to a burn whose cold, clear water pooled between

high banks. "Clean yourself up," Seyton ordered. A lady should be pleasing, not revolting. Even in her stupor she would probably not strip with him watching, so he led the pony to a mossy spot from which he could keep an eye on the high banks and make sure she couldn't escape, but where she could duck down out of his sight.

He was starving. Maybe there was food in the pack hanging from the pony's saddle.

. . . from the crown to the toe, top-full
Of direst cruelty!
ACT I, SCENE 5

MARY KICKED OFF HER USELESS SHOES, FULL OF HOLES FROM the day's hard walk, and plunged fully clothed into the water. It was frigid. She squealed in shock and dunked herself all the way under. Bending over, she dipped her hair up and down to scrub and rinse, and then scrubbed her body inside the wet tent of her gown, and scrubbed the gown last, leaving it on. When she came out of the water, the wind bit savagely through the wet material. She would freeze unless they started walking right now.

Her hair began to curl as soon as it began to dry, little tendrils and corkscrews lifting themselves. She swung her head to flip it behind her. The cold had somehow awakened her senses. She was not sure this was a good thing.

Seyton was sprawled on the ground eating Lady Macduff's oatcakes. He held up the pack. "The royal insignia," he said, "is cut into this leather."

"One of the princes left it behind in my room. I've been using it."

Seyton reached into the pack. Too late, she saw that he was snarling. Just so had Macbeth looked at Fleance the day that Banquo rode off to die.

Seyton pulled out the filthy trousers she had worn on her ride to Falkland. He flung them to the ground. Pulled out the tunic – the boots – the cap – and then hurled the pack after them. "It was *you*. On this pony! You little traitor. You rode to Lady Macduff to tell her to hide from me."

Mary almost clapped her hands. Lady Macduff *had* run to safety! She probably taunted Seyton from that impregnable tower, while he had to stand there on the grass and kick the children's toys. "She is just a woman," Mary reminded Seyton. "She doesn't matter to a king. And her babies need her. She didn't do anything wrong."

"Her husband is a traitor. If *Macduff* can't be made to pay the price for betraying Macbeth, *she* pays. Her husband knew that. Her husband made that choice."

Mary moved carefully. She retrieved the filthy clothes and put them back in the pack. She would wear the boots instead of her ruined shoes.

"Macbeth should have hanged you with your father," said Seyton. "But he and his lady were too kind. I'm not kind. I'll be your hangman."

Mary pulled on the boots.

Seyton now held Asleif's brooch in his hands. "Fleance gave this to you, didn't he?" said Seyton, shivering more than Mary, but with rage. "Think Fleance will rescue you, do you? You love that worm and not me, is that it?"

I should have stayed with Lady Macduff, thought Mary. I'd be safe now with her in that tower. But I thought I would be more useful back at the palace. I thought I could save others. I thought . . .

"I want your lands by rightful law, Lady Mary, so I'll wed you before I hang you. Tonight I'll ask Macbeth for my reward. Which is to marry you tonight."

Mary couldn't breathe. "Why do you deserve a reward?"

Seyton laughed.

"Lady Macduff?" she whispered.

"Dead," he said, smiling.

"And the children?"

He smirked.

"You killed the children?" she cried.

"I'll kill anything," said the man she had to marry.

Did heaven look on
And would not take their part?
ACT IV, SCENE 3

T HE HILL ON WHICH DUNSINANE STOOD WAS A THOUSAND FEET
high. One steep, crude path slanted up to the fortress.
It was a struggle for man and beast to climb that hill
even on the path. Off the path, the hill was raw with jagged
stone outcroppings, sharp cliffs, and deep gaps. Every tree had
been cut down so no one could creep unseen toward the
fortress.

The ancient stronghold had no windows, just arrow slots.
There was no lovely solar up there, no separate servants' quarters, no fine kitchens, no place to stroll. This was an army post. A
king did not come to Dunsinane to be loved by his people; he
came to Dunsinane to fight the enemy.

A cleft ran down the hillside, where at some ancient date there
had been a rockfall. Roots a hundred or a thousand years old
wrapped themselves around the stones. Tangled trees gave cover
through which no eye could see. Prince Malcolm and his officers
crept down the rockfall, threading through twisted birch and
dwarfed fir.

The English captains and the Scottish thanes talked of battle
plans and strategies. They wormed closer, gently moving branches
and studying Dunsinane through the leaves.

On the far side of Dunsinane, Fleance saw a thread of road stretching emptily toward the Sidlaw Hills. From his towers, Macbeth could see for miles.

"If we come out of Birnam Wood at the top of our hill," Siward was saying, "we'll have this long open slope to go down. We'll be within arrow range. If any of our men live to reach the bottom of the hill, they will now have to go up to Dunsinane. It'll take both hands to clamber up that rock face. No soldier will be able to hold a shield or sword."

Fleance knew what it was to need both hands. It was helplessness. It was defeat.

"Our only choice is to use the path, raising our shields over our heads for cover."

"Once we get up the path, though," said Lord Lennox gloomily, "the men won't be able to get any purchase on such a steep hill. We can't use a battering ram on the gate. We'll have no place to stand."

They stared at the impregnable fortress of the murderer, Macbeth.

Siward was a brilliant general. But even with ten thousand men attacking, would Dunsinane fall?

A serving boy had crept along after them, carrying the water. Now he took his leather casket from man to man, easing himself over rocks and roots, delivering a sip. Nobody saw him, because nobody ever really saw servants. The officers just drank the good, cold water.

"And even if we could carry ladders," said Lord Menteith, "there's no flat place to set them."

"Our ladders are too short anyway," said another. "We can't scale the wall."

"We have to coax Macbeth into open combat," said Prince Malcolm.

Lord Macduff shook his head. "He'll never do it. Why should he? Sitting there in that castle, he's safe. Out in the grass, he's at risk."

Far down that road that came to Dunsinane from the east, Fleance saw movement. He squinted to see who could possibly have decided to join Macbeth.

But the officers were distracted by someone inching through the underbrush, coming down from Birnam Wood to join them — yet another lord. In weeks past, Angus had come, then Lennox, Menteith, Caithness, and Macduff. What could it be like for Macbeth, as every thane who had sworn to him now went to the other side? Fleance hoped it was like hell.

Who should appear now but Lord Ross, who almost wept to see that Fleance was safe and well. They embraced as much as the terrain would allow. "Your father would be so glad you survived," said Lord Ross. "You are all that ever mattered to him, Fleance."

"Do you have any news?" demanded Prince Malcolm.

Ross let go of Fleance. "The tyrant just keeps killing. There are so many funerals the people hardly look up to ask who died." Then he sighed and turned to face Macduff. "What I have to say will not comfort you. My dear Duff, don't hate me for being the messenger. Macbeth had your wife and babes slaughtered. No one survived."

Macbeth shall never vanquished be until
Great Birnam Wood to high Dunsinane Hill
Shall come against him.
ACT IV, SCENE 1

MARY COULD SEE THE HILL THAT MUST BE DUNSINANE.

She trembled. Dark, looming walls seemed to spurt out of the bedrock. This was a terrible place where someone would come to a terrible end. When they got closer, she would probably see the arrow slits, but from here, the walls looked as slick and sightless as the inside of the hollow tree. It had but one tower, a square thuggish-looking thing, and below it, all the way around, a parapet that looked empty but wouldn't be.

Dunsinane was not a place for people to live. It was not even a place for people to fight. It was a place where people retreated.

Mary's heart collapsed at the thought of entering this place of siege and slaughter. The English would bring catapults to smash holes in these walls. Or undermine the foundations and tunnel under their feet. Or tip their arrows with tar and set them afire and soon the wooden roof would be blazing. And no one in either army cared if Mary of Shiel came out alive.

She looked beyond the grim fortress. Never had Mary seen a forest so deep, so dark. Through the night they would hear wildcats scream and wolves howl. Soon they would hear the drums of an attacking army, an army led by men whom once Macbeth had led.

Did Macbeth know that he, who had wanted the world, had ended up with the world against him?

Did Lady Macbeth know that she, who sold her soul for honor and glory, was cowering inside a great stone?

Your castle is surprised . . .
ACT IV, SCENE 3

I F I COULD GET INTO DUNSINANE," SAID FLEANCE, "I COULD OPEN THE gate for you."

They stared at him.

"How?" said Siward.

Fleance pointed. "Somebody's coming. One person on a horse and one person walking. I'll join them."

They looked skeptical.

"I'll say I'm a stable boy who got caught by the English troops and just now I managed to escape. I'll beg them to let me shelter inside with good King Macbeth."

Prince Malcolm shook his head. "Macbeth would recognize you, Fleance. He'd love to kill you. Remember he's already tried to murder you once. I have a duty to your father to keep you alive."

"I have a duty to my father to avenge him," said Fleance.

Macduff said ferociously, "*I'm* killing Macbeth. He's *mine.*"

But I'm finding the third murderer, thought Fleance. He's mine. I so swore, and I will so do. "I'll open the gate," he promised them, "and then all Macbeth's army will be yours."

They stripped off the fine clothing the English had found for Fleance. They put him in the dirty, worn clothes of the little water boy. Lennox rubbed leaf mold into Fleance's hair and over his face and neck, and then they splattered him with some of the water and muddied his face.

"A little blood helps," said Ross, slicing Fleance's arm before he knew it was happening and smearing the blood on his face and tunic. Then Ross tore off the sleeve and with the rag bound the wound he'd made.

"Godspeed!" they whispered, patting his shoulder.

He knew they did not expect to see him again. Nor did they expect him to open the gate. They would have another strategy. But he would keep his word. Two promises: one to his father's shade, one to his father's friends.

He crept on down. The ravine got shallower and had fewer trees, but it carried him to the very foot of the hill of Dunsinane. He crossed himself, took a deep breath, and burst out waving both arms at the two travelers coming toward him. Like a sheep, Fleance bleated, "Help me! Please!"

The rider was a man, wearing good clothes, while the walker was a woman, wearing rags. Any man wearing good clothes and going toward Macbeth was a noble in the enemy army, and Fleance could not risk being recognized. He stumbled, tugging respectfully at his forelock and cap while hiding behind his hand and keeping the cap low. Then he turned so he was facing Birnam Wood. He pointed to the top of the hill, so the noble's eye would land higher than where the tangle of officers and Prince Malcolm were hidden. "Full of Englishmen, sir! Danger, sir! I'm a stable boy. The horse I tended went lame, and I fell behind. The English caught me! I got away, but I got hurt. Please take me with you into the castle."

The noble did not care whether a stable boy got hurt. "How many men?" he demanded.

"Too many to count, sir." Fleance started running toward Dunsinane.

"Are they planning to attack right now?" asked the man.

"I don't think so, sir. I think a siege. They're talking of engines." Fleance was panting already. The hill was very steep.

The man laughed. Fleance knew that laugh. "Nobody can take Dunsinane by siege," said Seyton. "No English strategy matters. Dunsinane cannot fall until Birnam Wood actually moves. The Weird Ones said so. And since trees don't move, any more than hell ices over, Dunsinane is forever safe. So you and I, Lady Mary," he said, with venom, "we have time for a wedding this evening, don't we?"

Fleance stumbled, caught himself, and ran on.

To get inside Dunsinane, he was using the two people in Macbeth's court who most wanted him dead.

CHAPTER 13

... let us speak
Our free hearts each to other.
ACT I, SCENE 3

S EYTON BELLOWED A COMMAND, AND THE GATE BEGAN TO OPEN.
The hinges were still creaking when the great voice of
Macbeth came from the battlements: "Seyton! Get up
here! Tell me the news!"

Seyton slid off Mary's pony and handed the reins to the person he thought was a stable boy. Briefly, Seyton's hand touched
Fleance's. The man's forearm bore an angry scab from a recent
wound.

Fleance kept his face averted from Lady Mary, praying not to
be noticed. He needed to spend time in the courtyard watching

the mechanism of the gate, counting up the number of sentries, and seeing exactly where they were posted. But Lady Mary snatched the reins out of Fleance's hand, gave them to the nearest soldier, and shoved Fleance in front of her. "You! Boy! There are errands to be run. Things to fetch for the Queen. Get going."

Fleance was surrounded by soldiers. Some of these men would recognize him. Some might even be his father's men. If they believed the story Macbeth had put out – that he, Fleance, had murdered his father – Banquo's soldiers would be the first to kill Fleance. He had no choice but to go where Lady Mary pushed him.

They entered the ground floor of the tower block, which could be separately defended if the enemy were to burst in the gate. The hall was packed with soldiers and gear. A narrow stone stair without rails clung to the side wall. The next floor could be reached only by going up single file. Fleance guessed that the tower had three floors and that the women would be on the top, out of the way of the soldiers and relatively safe. But Lady Mary did not go to the stair. She was headed for the kitchen, where even in these circumstances Fleance found the rich smell of cooking enticing.

Their passage was blocked by a steward carrying an armload of provisions out of a cellar. He left the cellar door open as he staggered toward the kitchen. "Downstairs," whispered Lady Mary, and she bundled Fleance into the cellar, shutting the door behind them.

The steward had left a torch burning, so Fleance could see quite well. The cellar was a queer place, built right into the rocks of the hill, so its floor and walls were pitted and craggy. A tiny spring burbled in one corner, puddling in a scummy depression. Fleance hoped this was not the only water source for Dunsinane.

"Fleance, what are you doing here?" Lady Mary demanded. "This is a terrible risk! Macbeth would as soon chop you in pieces as look at you!"

She had recognized him? And wasn't putting a knife through him? "I thought you felt the same way," he said. By torchlight, he took his first real look at her and was shocked. "Are you all right, Lady Mary? You're filthy! You're bruised! Has Seyton been hurting you? Why were you walking while he was riding? Did he hit you? I'll kill him."

"You have to kill him anyway," said Mary, "and for a larger reason. He was one of the murderers of your father."

Fleance pictured the hand that had given him the pony's reins. I gave him that wound, he thought. Seyton is the third murderer, against whom I am sworn.

"Seyton was proud to explain to me that *he* killed Asleif," Lady Mary told Fleance. "Seyton knifed Asleif in the back just so that my betrothed would die dishonorably. It is your duty, Fleance, not just to kill Seyton but to dishonor him. Make it painful and frightening and terrible and long! Because, Fleance, he also killed Lord Macduff's little chicks – sweet children playing in the grass – and poor Lady Macduff, too." Lady Mary poked among barrels and casks, apparently looking for a hiding place for Fleance. There were weapons here, piled high. Anything he needed to destroy Seyton was at hand. But he had a larger purpose – if there could be a larger purpose than avenging one's own murdered father. He must open the gates for the English army to come in, so that Scotland could be saved from Macbeth. He must not allow himself to spend his life taking one man when it was Scotland at stake.

"Now, Fleance, tell me what you're doing here," said Lady Mary. "Sensible people are running *from* Macbeth, not toward him."

Fleance said, "Will Seyton be able to do what he threatened? Marry you tonight?"

Lady Mary's toughness vanished. She looked frail and young and small. "I don't know. I have a plan, but I'm not sure it will work. Tell me first what your plan is. Do you hope to assassinate Macbeth? That cannot happen. The Weird Ones – and Fleance, they have the truth of everything, I can testify to it – said that no man born of woman can hurt Macbeth."

How like the evil sisters to phrase it, thought Fleance, so it means nothing and everything. *No man born of woman.*

It was difficult to find a place to stand. Wooden platforms had been built over the sharpest rocks, so that barrels and sacks could be safely laid on them. Fleance was perched on a tiny platform. Now he saw that it had a handle and bolts. He stepped off, pulled the handle, and opened a trapdoor. He and Mary peered in.

It was a shallow hole. Empty. Fleance was not sure what the purpose was.

At the top of the stairs, the cellar door creaked. Mary and Fleance looked at each other. They had forgotten the steward. Fleance had nowhere to go except the hole. There was hardly room to crouch. He curled up, and Mary lowered the lid and stood on it. Too late, Fleance wondered if he could actually trust Mary. Because he knew now what the hole was. A dungeon. And should Mary kick the bolt in place, Fleance would end his life here.

To the person coming down the stairs, Lady Mary said lightly, "I'm counting portions of dried fish. How long do we expect the siege to last?"

Seepage from the spring soaked into Fleance's clothes. He was going to sneeze.

Lady Mary said, "Where are the servants who should be doing this labor for you? You are far too distinguished to be lugging stores from cellars."

The voice of the steward was pleased. "There is chaos in the castle," he told her. "The officers who should be organizing this war have deserted our king and gone to the English. It is despicable that our king should suffer like this. Those of us who are loyal now have double the work."

The steward did not seem to wonder who Lady Mary was or even realize that she had arrived a day or two after everybody else. So the steward was right that there was chaos. Fleance would have to make use of that. But how?

And what plan did Lady Mary have? How would Fleance get to her so that they could exchange information? If there was one person whose sharp eyes would also recognize Fleance, it was Lady Macbeth, hawk that she was. Fleance did not dare get near the women's quarters.

"You first, my lady," said the steward. "I'll carry the torch."

"Why, thank you, sir," said Lady Mary, and Fleance heard

her soft footsteps on the stair. He feared the steward suspected something and would stay to look around, but that didn't happen. The man tromped heavily after Lady Mary. The door shut.

And the steward bolted the cellar door from the outside.

<hr>

. . . honor, love, obedience, troops of friends,
I must not look to have; but, in their stead,
Curses . . .
ACT V, SCENE 3

<hr>

THE KITCHEN WAS WELL RUN. MARY APPROVED OF THE ARRANGE-ments and the standard of cleanliness. I learned that much from Lady Macbeth, she thought and suffered a stab of sorrow for the woman she had so admired. "I'll take that posset to the Queen now," she said sharply.

The staff exchanged nervous glances. No one wanted to admit they hadn't prepared a posset. No one wanted to admit they didn't have the slightest idea who Mary was, either, in her wrinkled, dirty gown with her hair in disarray, men's boots, and her leather satchel. Mary frowned at them. "To soothe her sore throat?" she reminded them.

They stopped everything to fix a nice hot drink, full of honey and cinnamon. They were afraid, but whether of the Queen, the King, or the army outside, Mary could not tell. She took the drink, they bobbed curtsies, and she understood that the kitchen staff was afraid of *her*.

She laughed out loud, increasing their anxiety, and headed for the tower. She hadn't been here before, but she could assume that the ladies were ensconced on the upper level. As she went through the kitchen passage, she slid open the bolt on the cellar door. Fleance was on his own. She couldn't help him. Marriage to Seyton would not be much different from being hanged, and she preferred to avoid both. She could not ask Lady Macbeth to help her – the Queen was beyond helping anybody, and almost certainly would not have helped Mary anyway. Mary's only hope was to convince everyone that she – alive and unwed – was essential to the Queen's health.

Narrow steep stairs – more like little protruding ledges – went sharply up. The stairs were poorly lit, having no windows, just a slit here and there. If the worst happened, each floor could be defended just by pushing attackers off the stairs.

The next floor turned out to be sleeping quarters for the men, and access to the battlements, where she could hear Macbeth bellowing. Mary climbed on up and entered the royal chamber, which would double as the solar and provide sleeping for the ladies-in-waiting – if there were still any ladies-in-waiting.

Mary prayed to Saint Margaret and Saint Hilda to walk in with her, and they did.

Lady Ross was coaxing the Queen to lie down. "You rest, your highness," she was saying, "and keep this compress on your forehead. I'll find my harp and sing for us." At the sound of Mary's boots, Lady Ross turned fearfully toward the door. When she saw Mary, tears of relief sprang into her eyes.

The Queen lay on her back, holding the poultice over her eyes.

The room was a dreadful place, smaller than Mary would have expected. Some space was given over to great barrels for water, in case the siege reduced them to utter desperation. There was nothing pretty here, no decoration, nothing soft. This was not a castle for sitting on window seats and sighing at the beauty of the moon.

Lady Ross backed away from the motionless Queen and flung herself into Mary's arms, taking comfort, as if Mary were the woman in her thirties and Lady Ross the young girl. "I'm so glad you're here," she breathed. "There isn't anybody else. Even the Queen's servants are gone! All through that terrible march here, people just dropped out, fell away, melting into the hills. But are you all right, Mary dear? You look as if someone tried to drown you."

"I'm fine. Is the Queen well?" If the Queen didn't even recognize Mary, there was no hope that her plan would work.

"In these troubled times, which of us is well?" said Lady Ross.

Mary agreed with that. "The Queen has a fever?" asked Mary.

"She has a greater disease," said Lady Ross shortly.

Mary's heart sank. Plague? Pox?

"'Tis called the Evil," said Lady Ross. "Here. Take off that dreadful gown. We'll burn it in the fire. I have a beaker of hot water. Let me bathe you. Travel has stained you terribly." Lady Ross gave Mary an efficient and desperately needed wash. "Now I'm going to pop you into my green gown," she said. "You always look so nice in green, Mary. Let me fix your hair." Lady Ross loved to fix hair. Mary sat gratefully on a stool while Lady Ross brushed out the twigs.

"If you're not going to sing, Lady Ross," said the Queen nastily, like a child taunting a sister, "then I will."

Lady Ross dropped her hairbrush and reached for the harp. But the Queen chose one note and chanted in a singsong drone. "The *Thane* of *Fife* – he *had* a *wife.*"

She knows what happened to Lady Macduff, thought Mary. How could she know? Seyton hasn't made his report yet. Did the news come more swiftly than Seyton and I could travel? After all, he had to walk back to me, and we were slow on that pony. Or did the Queen know in advance what Seyton was told to do?

"And where is she now?" asked the Queen with a queer triumph. "The wife of the Thane of Fife?"

"Dead," whispered Lady Ross in Mary's ear. "Macbeth ordered Lady Macduff and *all their babies* killed. He sent Seyton to do it. Mary, I tried so hard to postpone your wedding to Seyton. He's a terrible man. But I didn't think even he would murder babies. And now my own Ross – the husband in whom I place my trust – has gone to England, too! What are these men thinking of, leaving their wives behind? I am a prisoner in this castle with Macbeth, a hellhound if there ever was one, and my husband sends me a note that he's joining Prince Malcolm! What about me and the children? Our children – the ones we left by themselves, unprotected? If Lady Macduff was murdered because *her* husband went to England, shouldn't my husband fear that *I* will be murdered when *he* goes to England?"

Men have their valor and glory to consider, thought Mary. Their families are not first. In just that way, I was not first with my father and Asleif. "Does Macbeth know yet that your husband fled?" She, too, whispered, although the Queen could not possibly hear; she was chanting loudly about the demise of Lady Macduff.

"No, but the English armies are just over the hill. Macbeth has spies everywhere. I'm sure he has a spy in Siward's army. He'll be informed that my husband defected, and then he'll kill me."

"Leave now," said Mary. "Do not wait one minute. I will make excuses to the Queen until she has forgotten to ask, just as she forgot to ask about all the others who left."

Lady Ross shook her head. "I tried to run when you disappeared. But a soldier caught me. He was very polite. He said I must have lost control of my horse and he would keep the reins in his hand so it wouldn't happen again. Mary, it's so frightening here. Macbeth prowls like a dog in the night, howling that nothing can hurt him now. Macbeth's men are more afraid of Macbeth than of the English army. They believe him both cursed and blessed; they believe no one can escape his wrath, so they obey everything without question and without delay. If I were some stable boy, perhaps I could slip through the army lines pretending to carry water or firewood, but how does a lady vanish?"

"With the clothing Prince Malcolm left behind. Come. You will be that very stable boy." Mary yanked a blanket off the pile by the bed and held it up for shelter. Lady Ross stepped out of her gown and into the muddy trousers. She lowered the filthy tunic over her fair shoulders and the soiled cap over her lovely hair. Mary wrapped her in the blanket and called to the Queen, "I'll be right back, your highness. I'm going down to the kitchen to get you a bite of supper."

The Queen was busy washing her hands.

The stairs were more frightening going down. Lady Ross was unfamiliar with trousers and fearful of tripping on the edges of the blanket. It was a mark of the general confusion that none of the soldiers milling around below wondered about these two peculiar creatures crawling down the wall. When at last they reached the ground floor, Mary whipped off the blanket, grabbed Lady Ross's arm as she had grabbed Fleance, and said sharply, "You do as you are told, young man!" She marched Lady Ross into the courtyard.

Mary had not realized just how tall the walls of Dunsinane were. From the outside, the power of this fortress was impressive enough, but here on the inside, she saw that it was also a prison.

Amazingly, Mary's pony was still there. Nobody had done anything about him. "I said," Mary scolded loudly, "that we need eggs for the Queen, and you are getting them! I don't care how far you have to ride. Get on that pony and come back with eggs."

Lady Ross mounted awkwardly, embarrassed by the trousers.

"Remember you're a boy," breathed Mary. "You're brave. You're fast." Leading the pony, Mary walked grandly to the gate, swishing the bright fabric of her gown, drawing attention to herself, and flinging her long, golden-red hair around her shoulders. "This stupid boy," she said to the sentry, "is going to find eggs for the Queen. Our dear queen isn't well. We're making her a pudding that will go down easily. Open that gate. Stop whining about it. It's one boy on one pony. The gate will be open one moment. You're perfectly safe, you lily-livered toad. Hurry up."

The bar across the gate was as big as a tree. Fixed into position, it not only stretched across the two great doors but also spread down the thick stone walls, supported by great iron sockets. But both the bar and the iron had been oiled, and two men easily slid it back. They opened a crack exactly wide enough for the chunky little pony. "Don't you let the Queen down!" Mary snapped at poor Lady Ross, and she smacked the pony's flank to make it run.

The pony did not even consider running down so steep and rough a hill. It slowly picked its way. Macbeth and Seyton and every other soldier on those battlements had only to glance down and they would see what was happening and seize poor Lady Ross and kill her. "Close the gate!" Mary ordered the sentries. "Don't be so careless."

This is the very painting of your fear.
This is the air-drawn dagger . . .
ACT III, SCENE 4

A WEDDING?" SHOUTED MACBETH. HE HURLED HIS BEER JUG AT Seyton. "You have interrupted me to ask about your *wedding?* Do you think I care about *women* at a time like this? You whey-faced loon." The King stormed around the ramparts, checking every stone, every corner.

Seyton followed.

The King was riveted by Birnam Wood. Seyton himself couldn't see much but trees. It was a large area, he knew, royal lands kept for hunting. When this was over, Seyton would arrange a hunt. He loved hunting, and it was far too long since they'd had a good chase. Killing deer wouldn't leave him with these sticky hands the way killing those . . . He stopped the remembrance.

"You bungled killing Fleance along with his father," said Macbeth contemptuously. "Did you accomplish killing that woman and all the children? News came from a neighbor of Falkland, but I want it from you. I don't want heirs left, do you understand?"

"Yes, sir. There are no heirs left, sir."

Macbeth forgot the children. He looked back out at Birnam Wood. "They're out there."

"Yes, sir."

"They can't get me," said the King.

"No, sir," said Seyton. "Remember how your sword smoked that day against Macdonwald? And then, you were only Thane of Inverness and Glamis. Now you're king!" Seyton started to add that God would be on Macbeth's side, because Macbeth was king, but the words tripped him up. Why, then, had God not been on Duncan's side? And even though Macbeth had been righteously crowned at Scone, there was nothing righteous in his kingship.

It was not going to be God on Macbeth's side. It was going to be witches.

Macbeth chanted, quoting the witches, "'I laugh at the power of man, because none of woman born shall harm Macbeth.'"

"The three Weird Ones on the heath told you?" Seyton asked.

"The same. Have you seen them?"

"And brought gifts to them," said Seyton. "How large was your gift?"

Macbeth was startled. "I brought nothing. I am King. I demanded."

Seyton would have said that evil powers always required gifts and from a king would require kingly gifts.

"This crown sears my eyeballs," said Macbeth.

There was not enough sun to squint at, and the King's head was bare. Seyton looked around for an explanation, as if he might see a crown nearby. Instead he saw Lady Mary, in a vivid green gown, capturing the eyes of an army as she sashayed across the courtyard, while down the steep path outside the gate, that stable boy was riding away.

~~~

We have scotched the snake, not killed it.
ACT III, SCENE 2

~~~

FLEANCE LIFTED THE LID WITH A GROAN, UNBENT HIMSELF, AND climbed out. He was wet and smelled mossy, but at least he wasn't permanently sealed in a dungeon. Thanks to Mary he could get out of here, and he had better do it fast, before the steward spotted that open bolt.

Where could he stand so that he could see everything, learn what he needed to know about the gate and the troops, yet not be seen by anybody who might recognize him? How would he know when to open that gate? How would he signal Prince Malcolm that it was time to rush the castle?

If he opened it too soon, Macbeth's men would shut it again and kill him.

If he waited too long, and Siward's troops were already coming up the path, Macbeth's men would stand on the ramparts right over that very gate, pouring boiling oil down on the attackers, and Fleance would be responsible for the slaughter.

There was another problem. If Fleance were caught, Seyton would know that Lady Mary had something to do with Fleance getting in. So if I am caught, I am dead, thought Fleance, and so is Lady Mary.

He left the narrow kitchen passage, sauntered through the hall, and came out into the courtyard. He looked around for horses so he could spend time watering and grooming and especially shoveling manure, because nobody ever wanted to do that, and they weren't going to interrupt boys who were.

He was just in time to see Lady Mary send some *other* boy off on her pony. She was yelling about eggs.

Fleance was mystified.

Seyton came storming down a wide set of stairs that gave access from the courtyard to the battlements. Fleance pretended to be busy unhitching an ox team, although what he would do with them afterward, he didn't know. He kept low, studying the fortress.

"Why did you let that stable boy go?" Seyton shouted at the guards.

Fleance yearned to be driving a stake through the man's heart, and instead he had to hide behind an ox.

"Lady Mary said to. He's getting eggs for the Queen, so Lady Mary can fix a nice egg pudding for the Queen's sore throat."

Seyton opened his mouth to scream about this, too, but Macbeth had followed him down and seemed pleased with Lady Mary's plan, and yet startled, as if he had forgotten he had a queen, let alone one with a sore throat. Up the stairs to visit his wife Macbeth went, with Seyton at his heels and Lady Mary close behind.

She was a completely different person from the grubby, soiled girl who had hidden him in the cellar. She was a woman, her hair loosely caught by a kerchief, spilling in bright array on her shoulders, catching the eye of a hundred men who would like a woman like this.

Fleance could not bear to think about her in the company of those evil men, soon to be trapped in the bedroom of an equally evil woman.

Soldiers were huddled near the ox team. They jerked their heads at Macbeth. "If he's blessed by God, I'm Saint Margaret," said one sourly.

"They say Prince Malcolm's out there," said another.

"What's going on outside? Does anybody know?"

"Who can see from here? Only the officers and those on watch get to have a look at this Birnam Wood they're so excited about."

"They say England will attack soon."

"They say Malcolm is the rightful king, and rightful kings always win."

"I don't like being trapped in here, where we can't see."

Fleance fastened the ox team back up again. Then he eased

into a group of soldiers. "I'm mending and cleaning," he said cheerfully. "Anyone have trousers or tunics for me?"

The men were happy to have anything happen, they were so bored, and went through their packs to hand over old clothes. It was a nice selection from which Fleance could now dress as a soldier. He'd be wearing Macbeth's colors, not a happy prospect, but he might be able to draw sentry duty.

At the gate.

Finger of birth-strangled babe
Ditch-delivered by a drab:
Make the gruel thick and slab.
ACT IV, SCENE 1

THE KING OF SCOTLAND HAD EXACTLY ONE LORD STILL WITH him: Seyton, who should have been very low on a list of nobles.

The Queen of Scotland had exactly one lady-in-waiting: Mary, who was not on the list at all, being the daughter of the traitor Cawdor.

"I will stay by the Queen's side," Mary said to Macbeth, although she had not the slightest intention of doing so. "Have you a physician who could tend to her?" If there was a doctor, he might give the Queen a sleeping potion (the only thing doctors could be counted on to do), and Mary could slip away in the night.

The King seemed to take note that his wife was in a desperate situation. He ordered Seyton to find a doctor. But the best medicine – his presence – he did not think of. He left for the parapet, where he could go on studying Birnam Wood.

The Queen washed her hands. The fingers were so red and chapped she might have been a scullery maid herself. Her lovely hands had open, infected sores. Mary took the jar of lanolin and began to massage the soft, sweet-smelling lotion into those poor hands.

"Blood," explained the Queen.

"No," said Mary, wanting to weep for her even when she knew what kind of woman this really was; wanting her to be beautiful once more, in body and in soul. "It's a balm, to heal you."

Mary was astonished when a kitchen maid from Inverness entered the room, carrying a large covered tray of hot food. It could not have been easy to climb those horrid stairs balancing that heavy tray. The girl was one of the staff from Inverness, but Mary couldn't even remember her name.

"Jennet," said the girl, curtsying to the Queen, who did not notice her. Mary set the Queen's hands in her lap and followed the girl to the stairs. Please let there be allies here. "Jennet," she said casually, "is anybody else here from Inverness? Did Swin come back? Or Ildred?"

"Swin never come back. She knows how to live in the woods nor ever be seen. Like her name."

"Her name?"

"Swin. Means one swine. Like a wild boar, that girl is. Tusks."

Mary had thought it was the old word for swan. She saw now

that Swin was both: the savage wild beast and the elegant white swimmer.

"Nor Ildred won't ever be back, either. Father Ninian came for her."

"He did?" Mary was delighted. "He's all right? She's all right?"

Jennet looked at her incredulously. "How could she be all right? After her having that baby, Ildred thought the father would marry her, but he laughed. Took the babe, though. Promised Ildred he'd find it a good home."

Oh, poor Ildred! That she had a baby and nobody knew nor cared enough to wonder why she got heavy. Nobody noticed her pain and travail. And that included Mary, who had tried to stay as far from Ildred as possible. "Why didn't she tell Lady Macbeth?" asked Mary, thinking that way back then, in another world and another time, Lady Macbeth would have ordered the man to marry Ildred.

"Because Ildred sinned, tempting a man and having a baby without getting married. The lady would have thrown her out on the moor to live like a leper. Father Ninian found out too late to help. He was caring for his flock, you know, it's why he couldn't leave Inverness when we did. But Ildred needed him, so he came for her."

"Ildred is fine, then," said Mary. "I'm so glad."

"Fine?" said Jennet scornfully. "Seyton — as you're going to wed, lady — was the father of that baby. The witches needed a baby's fingers for their brew, and he brought them. And you think Ildred is fine?"

CHAPTER 14

This disease is beyond my practice.
ACT V, SCENE 1

THE QUEEN WAS UP ALL NIGHT, WRITING LITTLE NOTES TO HERSELF, washing her hands, and swaying in front of flickering candles. She could not set fire to this cavern of stone, but she could easily set her own gown alight. Mary extinguished the candles and hid them. In the icy dark she lay shivering in mind and body.

In the morning, Mary fussed over the Queen's hair and bathed the Queen's body, fed the Queen's mouth and laced the Queen's gown. "We're going for a walk," said Mary, who could not abide this cell another hour.

The Queen's eyes grew bright at the sight of those awful stairs, and Mary's fear was not that the Queen would be afraid to walk down. It was that the Queen might willingly step off into the air.

At last they safely reached a courtyard packed with men, weapons, and wagons. Mary and Lady Macbeth threaded through the obstacles of war. "Come spring," said Mary brightly, "we could plant roses here. How warm and sheltered they would be against this nice south-facing wall. See where the wall juts out – wouldn't this be a perfect niche for a statue? Perhaps of a favorite saint. Which saint should we choose?"

Lady Macbeth dusted her hands free of saints – who had probably in the same fashion dusted themselves free of Lady Macbeth.

Searching all the while for Fleance, Mary stumbled instead over the King and Seyton. The Queen looked at her husband in an agony of desire and held out a trembling hand. By daylight, Macbeth could not avoid seeing her terrible state – hair faded, skin blotchy, eyes fevered. "Where's that doctor?" shouted the King. "Find him! Mary! Take her upstairs. She needs to be in bed."

Back they went, and Mary knew that, this time, there would be no coming out. Mary would be a prisoner in this tower as Lady Macbeth was a prisoner of her deeds.

The doctor scurried in, wringing his hands and tiptoeing around.

"Unnatural deeds result in unnatural troubles," he muttered to Mary.

It *was* unnatural to murder people. "But the King will want to see you doing something," she pointed out.

He poured Lady Macbeth a tot of this and a dram of that, dosing it heavily with honey and cinnamon so it would slide down easily, but not as if he thought anything would come of it. He held it to her lips, and she seemed to swallow. "Mandrake," the doctor said, watching his patient. He set down the beautiful cup that had meant so much to Lady Macbeth in another lifetime, at Inverness. "She needed only one swallow. It gives a very heavy sleep."

And indeed, in minutes, the Queen was sprawled on her back, arms flung out, gown in disarray, mouth hanging open. Mary pitied her and rolled her on her side, folding her arms down, so she would look less like a slattern.

Macbeth sprang into the room, followed by Seyton and a horde of anxious soldiers. Mary did not think they were anxious about the Queen.

"The patient?" demanded Macbeth. "How do you plan to help her?"

"She is troubled by fancies that keep her from rest," said the doctor carefully.

"Well, cure her!" the King shouted. "You must have some medicine for a diseased mind, some antidote to cleanse her heart." Macbeth glared at everyone in turn. Everyone tried to be invisible. "Throw medicine to the dogs, anyway," said Macbeth angrily.

The doctor panicked. Did the King intend to throw *him* to the dogs?

"My lord," said someone from the stairs, "we have a report from the English camp. They're on the move."

A shiver went through the room. Heads bowed, hands

trembled, cheeks paled. Men wet their lips and looked around for something stronger to wet their lips with.

Macbeth's fury swung from the doctor to his men. "Seyton!"

"Sir."

"Hang any man who shows fear."

Everyone rushed around, stupid with the fear they had been ordered not to have. There was nothing anybody could do anyway. They could only wait for England to attack.

But Macbeth had already forgotten them. "Tomorrow, and tomorrow, and tomorrow," he said, as if he could see each long worthless day stretching in front of him, "creeps at this petty pace, to the last syllable of recorded time."

Mary shuddered.

"Life's but a walking shadow. A poor player that struts and frets his hour upon the stage and then is heard no more."

This had been true for Mary's father. His hour was gone, and no one even remembered his name.

Macbeth went to the angled alcove whose window slit faced Birnam Wood. "Life is a tale told by an idiot," he said to his enemies. "Full of sound and fury, signifying nothing." He clattered back down the stairs, his men following. After dithering for a few minutes, the doctor rushed out, too.

Mary called after them, although they could not hear, because fear of the coming attack had hit the troops, and a rising clamor was filling the castle. "You're wrong! Life is a privilege. We write our own tales. We do not have to be steeped in blood. We can choose to be steeped in kindness. You may have surrounded me with sound and fury, my lord, but I will find peace and joy. You may have withered on a blasted heath, but I will make a home and have love."

The Queen of Scotland laughed.

⌒

A drum, a drum!
Macbeth doth come.
ACT I, SCENE 3

⌒

THE MEN HAD SLEPT IN SHIFTS ON THE COURTYARD FLOOR, OR IN THE hall, or on the floor above. When they were not sleeping, they had nothing to do except worry. Now they moved in little knots, muttering, praying, swearing.

"We're blind down here," Fleance complained. "We can't see a thing. How do we know what's happening?"

After a moment, he joined another group. "We're blind down here," he said to them. "We can't see a thing past those walls and this gate. How do we know what's happening?"

He circled the entire courtyard and arrived back where he had started.

The men said to him, "We're blind down here. We can't see a thing past those walls and this gate. How do we know what's happening?"

⌒

Let every soldier hew him down a bough . . .
ACT V, SCENE 4

ALCOLM POSITIONED THE ENGLISH ARMY AT THE CREST OF the hill, standing invisibly just inside Birnam Wood. "If only the trees went all the way down the hill," he lamented. "Then we'd have cover."

Mist rolled in, thick fleecy handfuls attached by threads, shifting and lifting.

"But of course," said Malcolm, son of Duncan. "The woods *can* go all the way down the hill. Let every soldier cut the bough of a tree and hold it in front of him. Through this mist, through those branches, Macbeth won't see an army. He'll see Birnam Wood."

. . . our poisoned chalice
To our own lips . . .
ACT I, SCENE 7

ARY NEEDED TO BE PREPARED.
She checked the prince's satchel, making sure the knife was there. She tested the sharpness of the blade against her thumb. Then she tucked it under the leather

fold and put the satchel against the wall where, in the shadowy unlit room, it was almost impossible to see.

The Queen's eyes were open. Better that the poor woman should sleep through the coming attack. Mary lifted the royal cup and supported the Queen's head, and the Queen obediently swallowed more mandrake potion. Then Mary poured two cups of wine and set them on the little table by the Queen's bed.

Sure enough, Macbeth sent Seyton to check on the Queen. Mary gave him her best smile. "I am glad for your company. The Queen is ill, and I am so worried. But she sleeps at last. You may reassure the King that she is at ease."

Seyton stood over the Queen. She was difficult to recognize.

"Seyton, please forgive my behavior," said Mary, trembling up at him. "Please forgive my silly lies. It was panic and fear. I know you would never panic or fear. But I am a weaker vessel."

He folded his arms and regarded her silently.

"A cup of wine with me?" she said. "We've a store here of the finest wines ever presented to a King, and no one to share them with. You and I could drink to each other." She handed him the Queen's cup and sipped from her own. If he drank, he would collapse. She would kill him with the prince's knife. Could she do it? She had to. So many deaths and so much pain had to be avenged.

Horror filled her. She did not want to do this. She wanted a stainless soul.

But Mary had not enticed him by the false courage of drink. "We're going out on the battlements," said Seyton. "You will ask the King to wed us. Right now. Something might happen to you," he added, smiling his beautiful smile, "and I want to be a rich widower when it does."

He made Mary go first. He wouldn't push her off the side yet because he needed the marriage to happen. But it was not pleasant to have him at her back as she edged down the stair ledges.

She had not been out on the battlement until now.

Dunsinane was on a much higher hill – a peak, really – than Inverness or Forres had been. Yet Mary could not see very far, because they were surrounded by a sea of woods. There was no trace of English troops. Maybe the attack was false rumor, and Macbeth was right, and this awful waiting would continue tomorrow, and tomorrow, and tomorrow.

Seyton's fingers dug into her arm, reminding her of her task. When we're wed, he'll throw me over the parapet, thought Mary.

It was an appalling drop: sheer stone walls, sheer rock face, and, at the bottom, a jagged jumble of crags and stumps. Her mouth went dry, and her hands went clammy. She turned aside from that terrible edge and looked down instead into the courtyard.

Fleance, all too visible from above, was organizing a rebellion, touching a shoulder here and clapping a back there. If Macbeth or Seyton saw him now, he was dead. She must provide a diversion! She must –

A slow, eerie tapping came from the hills.

Every man in Dunsinane froze.

The tapping picked up speed and settled into a steady *rat-a-tat-tat*.

For a full minute, one war drum played alone, announcing the plan. Then another drum joined, and another, until Dunsinane vibrated with the throbbing of a hundred drums.

Macbeth rushed from corner to corner, staring at Birnam Wood. But nothing was out there.

Every heart trapped in Dunsinane was trapped now in the beat of enemy drums. Every pulse stepped up to the pace set by wooden sticks. A thousand hearts were beating, beating, beating.

On the hills, not a leaf moved. Not a flag blew. Not a soldier stood.

Just drums drumming.

A raw, sobbing cry interfered with the horrible repetition of the drums.

"What's that?" demanded Macbeth. "It's coming from the Queen's room. Seyton. Go see what happened."

Our castle's strength
Will laugh . . .
ACT V, SCENE 5

ALL THESE DRUMS," FLEANCE KEPT SAYING. "WHY DO THE OFFICERS tell us that nothing is happening? It sounds like ten thousand soldiers to me. Why don't they tell us the truth?"

The thin, relentless drum-chatter made the men breathe faster. They were panting now, reaching for water but finding the beer

Fleance had been rolling out, barrel after barrel. The *rat-a-tat-tat* demanded action. Drinking was a kind of action.

"Unless it's witches," Fleance pointed out. "They say Macbeth goes to witches. Could be that this isn't the English army. Could be those drums are playing by themselves."

In the courtyard, they began to wonder: Were those drums strapped to the chests of little English drummer boys? Or hanging in the air, playing to the unsung tunes of witches?

"We'll be the last to know, won't we?" said Fleance. "Down here with fifty feet of stone going up and twelve feet of stone going out, and no way to see, and no way to get ready, and no way to brace ourselves. But there's always the gate. We could open the gate. Then we'd see. Then we'd know. Witches or war?"

. . . anon, methought
The wood began to move.
ACT V, SCENE 5

EVERY ONE OF MALCOLM'S SOLDIERS WANTED THICK LEAFY BRANCHES, which would look the most treelike and attract the fewest arrows. Some chose fir and some birch, others oak and sycamore.

The whisper was given to begin moving.

The men were amazed.

They were trees.

Their boots felt like roots and their hands like leaves. They started walking and feared to stop, lest when the time came to drop these branches, it would be impossible, because they would have sprouted and turned to timber.

. . . by self and violent hands
Took off her life . . .
ACT V, SCENE 8

THE KING OF SCOTLAND NO MORE SAW MARY THAN HE SAW THE separate stones of the turret. A weird mist had settled over the opposite hill, like snow or fleece. Mary's mind felt just as thick. When Seyton came back again, he seemed to stumble. He did not see Mary, either. He approached the King as if they had never met.

"What do you want?" snapped Macbeth.

"The Queen, my lord, is dead."

Mary was stunned. But Lady Macbeth was merely thin and anxious! Surely not on the brink of death!

Macbeth – who had been more in love with his wife than any man Mary had ever known – Macbeth shrugged. "She should have died hereafter. Get my armor, Seyton."

The King's armor was piled near the bed he did not share with his queen. Mary followed Seyton into the royal chamber. He stared down at the King's armor as if he no longer recognized its purpose, and Mary inched closer to the Queen.

Lady Macbeth had stabbed herself. Her hand was still wrapped around the knife with which she had pierced her heart. It was the dirk from Mary's pack. So the mandrake root had not put her to sleep. She had seen Mary take out the knife and test the blade. The knife of Prince Malcolm, whose own father had been stabbed to death by Macbeth – or by this lady herself.

"So she's dead," said Seyton, looking down at the corpse. "It's for the best."

Best, thought Mary. Oh, my poor Lady Macbeth, who so wanted the best! Who wanted it today and could not wait for tomorrow. Death is your best.

Blow wind, come wrack,
At least we'll die with harness on our back!
ACT V, SCENE 5

SEYTON DRESSED HIS KING FOR BATTLE, CAREFULLY TIGHTENING HERE, adjusting there, making sure the shoulder straps were comfortable and that no sharp edge rubbed against the King's skin. A soldier dashed up to them and stood beside them and began gasping in an awful dragging sort of way. Seyton thought the man must have an arrow through his lungs, so he ducked below the parapet to protect his own chest.

"Lord," whispered the soldier, trying to breathe, trying to point. *"Birnam Wood is moving."*

Seyton peered over the rampart.

Trees were edging closer, inch by inch, foot by foot, root by root, spreading down the hill.

Birnam Wood was moving.

Seyton was transfixed.

"The trees!" screamed a terrified voice. "They move! They walk! All those drums are not the drums of men and armies. They are the drums of witches! It's *trees* advancing on us!"

One sentry panicked. He tried to open the gate. Others quickly sprang to his aid.

Seyton came to his senses. He bellowed to the officers below. "Stop that soldier! Do not open those gates!"

He raced down the stairs and into the courtyard. The men pressed against Seyton as if to squash the news out of him. "What's happening?" they shouted. "What are those trees they're talking about?"

"Nothing. The English are coming," he said, as if he hadn't just watched a forest drift from its roots.

But from some high and lonely place the cry of horror continued. "The trees are sliding down the mountain!"

"We've got to see!" shouted one soldier.

"Open the gates!"

"We're blind down here!"

Seyton grabbed the shoulder of the stupid little kern who had started this and swung him around, prepared to smash his jaw, show who was in charge.

Fleance, son of Banquo.

The devil damn thee black...
ACT V, SCENE 3

FLEANCE HAD KNOWN THIS WAS A GAMBLE. HAD KNOWN HE MIGHT lose. But he had been so close. Now Seyton had him pinned against the very gate he had thought to open.

I failed, he thought. Oh, Father! I thought to give Scotland a good king again! I thought to open gates and save lives and even to avenge you. And I failed.

"To think little Lady Mary got you inside Dunsinane," said Seyton. "She's smarter than she looks. But when I'm done with her, she won't have any looks." Seyton turned Fleance over to soldiers so strong they hardly noticed the slender weight of the boy.

"Into the hall," directed Seyton.

The hall was empty of soldiers, because they had all gone out to fight. Carefully working their way up the treacherous stairs were two muscular men holding either end of an empty coffin. Lady Mary was above them, beckoning. "All the way up to the royal chamber," she was saying. "We won't put the Queen's body in yet. I haven't bathed her."

"Well, well," said Seyton. "I have both of you. And in the presence of such a favorable omen – a coffin. Up after them, Fleance." He smiled and drew his sword.

Mary lifted her chin and said in the voice of a lady – albeit a defeated lady – "You will permit me to do one last thing for our

queen, Seyton. I cannot leave her body to be defiled by her enemies. She has taken herself to hell, but I can ward off that final
insult. You will give me time to prepare my queen."

The coffin carriers had achieved a certain momentum to get
up those steep ledges and were lunging forward. Lady Mary
backed up. Fleance was forced to follow.

"You were so paltry-looking, Fleance, that I didn't even bother
with you," said Seyton. "That's how you got away the night I
killed your father."

They reached the top floor. Grunting, the laborers lugged the
coffin over next to the Queen's bed. It was a warrior's coffin.
Many such would be needed today. It was not lined in plush or
silk nor was it pillowed for a queen. It was just a box waiting for
a body.

Open locks,
Whoever knocks!
ACT IV, SCENE 1

THE SOLDIERS IN THE FORECOURT WATCHED SEYTON GO.
They hated Seyton.
They hated even more that nobody was telling them
what was happening.

"That kern he dragged off had the right idea."

"What are we supposed to do, stand here all day and wait and
not see anything?"

"Open the gate."

"What if the English army is there?"

"They keep telling us it's just trees. Open the gate!"

<hr/>

... against his murderer shut the door ...

ACT I, SCENE 7

<hr/>

MARY TOUCHED THE HEAVY HARDWARE ON A COFFIN designed to seal a body forever in the grave. There had been no Mass of the dead for Banquo, and she did not think there would be one for Lady Macbeth. She wept for the Queen, who had been good once, or so Mary hoped.

And then, over the *rat-a-tat-tat* of the drums, blared the fanfares of trumpets. The English were proclaiming victory for a battle not yet fought.

How could it sound to Macbeth? His castle surrounded by trumpet calls, like in the Bible when Joshua made the walls of Jericho fall.

The soldiers below were screaming that God had forsaken them.

Mary did not believe that God ever walked away. But men on earth could be sufficiently evil that God could not be reached through the blood mist of their deeds.

The coffin carriers fled. Seyton's two men continued to hold on to Fleance. Seyton smiled at Mary. "Which is your bed?"

Mary waved her cup at the narrow low mattress across the room.

"Fleance will enjoy watching this," said Seyton. He lifted the Queen's cup, all studded with gems and gold.

Drink it, drink it! Mary willed.

"I'll take my marriage privileges now," said the third murderer.

"Show some reverence," said Mary. "The Queen lies here."

"Won't be looking, will she?" Seyton waved the cup around the room instead of swallowing the contents. "I lead a charmed life," he said. "The King wants you dead, Fleance, but I'll save you for Macbeth to play with after his victory. 'Here, sir,' I'll say. 'A little dog for you to kick.'"

Fleance thought of his father's list of dogs. He could not die a spaniel. But neither could he free himself from the grip of the two soldiers.

"Macbeth will lose the battle," said Mary.

"He won't," said Seyton. "He went to the witches for help, and they promised him."

"They promised *something*," said Mary. "But what?"

The soldiers were shaken. "Witches? Macbeth forsook God? Our army is controlled by witches?"

From below came a huge swelling chaos of sound, the screaming of a thousand throats and the stomping and pounding of feet and weapons, and the clear, distinctive creak of hinges.

"The gates are open," cried one of the soldiers. "They've opened the gates to the enemy! The enemy's here."

No, thought Fleance. The enemy is *here*.

The men dropped their grip on him, rushing down to join the fight. Fleance leaped forward. He was barehanded against Seyton and he was half Seyton's size, but he had twice the rage and all the right. Fleance hoped to disable Seyton's right hand, his weapon hand. Then he would use Seyton's own sword and dirk against him.

Fleance caught Seyton's wrist. With his entire weight, he drove the arm backward, angling to dislocate the shoulder or snap the bones in his arm.

He wasn't strong enough. He could immobilize Seyton, but not break the bones. They were locked together, grunting. Seyton's free hand found Fleance's throat.

Lady Mary seized the handle of Seyton's sword. She yanked it out, raking it hard against Seyton's flesh and slicing him open. She wasn't strong enough to kill him, but she could certainly give Fleance time to do such.

Seyton was no fool. He dropped heavily to the floor, which knocked Mary backward so she could not use the sword. But this did not shake Fleance's grip on his right arm. Seyton gave up trying to strangle Fleance, but with his left hand – his awkward, untrained left – he pulled out his dirk.

Fleance let go of Seyton's wrist, and jumped high into the air, ramming the heels of his boots upon the blade just as Seyton had switched it into his right hand.

The impact of Fleance's boots shoved the blade through Seyton's fingers. The fingers of his killing hand tumbled to the floor, one more offering to the forces of evil.

"Go, Mary," said Fleance, taking the sword. "I will finish this.

Lock yourself in the kitchen with the serving girls. You and they will be safest there. Run. There is little time."

She ran.

Beware Macduff;
Beware the Thane of Fife.
ACT IV, SCENE 1

THE MIDDLE FLOOR WAS EMPTY. SHE RAN ACROSS IT TO THE NEXT SET of stairs, first peering down the stair hole into the hall. Also empty. Mary flattened herself against the wall and flew down the treacherous ledges, across the hall, and into the serving passage, and a roar filled the hall behind her.

"Turn around, you hellhound!"

It was the voice of Macduff. And in this castle of Dunsinane, there was but one hellhound: Macbeth.

But Macduff must not fight Macbeth, thought Mary. The Weird Ones have been right about everything. They'll be right about this. Macbeth cannot be harmed by a man born of woman. It's Macduff who will die.

Mary wept for all the senseless dying of all these awful months. She did not flee to the kitchen. She turned, sadly and heavily, to watch the duel between a wicked king and a doomed thane.

Dunsinane went silent.

Fighting died away.

Trumpets ceased to speak, and drums ceased to roll.

"Get away from me," muttered Macbeth. "I have enough blood of Macduffs on my hands."

"You admit you murdered my wife and chicks?"

"You'll be killed, not I," said Macbeth, tiredly. "No man born of woman can harm me."

"I was not born," said Macduff, Thane of Fife, Lord of Falkland. "I was cut out of my mother's womb."

The sword of Macduff plunged into the King.

. . . sighs and groans, and shrieks that rent the air . . .
ACT IV, SCENE 3

FLEANCE PRICKED SEYTON'S THROAT WITH THE SWORD.

Seyton whimpered. He could not look at his own wound, where his fingers had been severed from his hand.

"Get up," said Fleance. "I'm going to bind your hand and keep you for Macbeth. You'll be the dog he kicks."

Seyton got up, gripping his ruined hand as if covering it up would keep it from being real.

With the sword tip, Fleance pushed him until the backs of Seyton's knees were pressed against the open coffin. Then he shoved the sword forward into Seyton's gut until Seyton, trying to get away, fell backward rather neatly into the coffin of Lady Macbeth.

"You said you'd keep me alive!" screamed Seyton.

Fleance slammed down the lid and shot the bolts. "And so I will," he said.

Inside the coffin Seyton sobbed in fear and kicked against heavy boards that would never yield.

Fleance spoke through the coffin boards. "It could be worse, Seyton. You could be lying out in the woods somewhere, with twenty gashes in you, like my father. Or left for the foxes, like the innocent chicks of Lord Macduff. But no, you're warm and dry in a sealed coffin."

"Please! Let me out!"

"The battle is noisy. No one will hear you. But when the hurly-burly is done, somebody will probably come up here. They'll open this door. They'll smell the stink of Lady Macbeth's corpse and see it lying on her bed – and when you scream – well, Seyton, who wants to be in the same room with a corpse that screams? No one, Seyton. They'll slam the door and run away, and no one, ever, not even for a minute, will come up here again."

"No! Have mercy!" came the muffled shriek.

"You will die in pain. Slowly and without honor. That fulfills a promise I made," said Fleance. He left, going down the stairs, not noticing that they were dangerous but only that they led to Mary. The middle floor of the tower was empty, but in the hall below, Prince Malcolm, General Siward of England, and all the minor thanes – Ross and Angus, Menteith and Caithness – were staring at Macduff.

The body of Macbeth lay at his feet.

Fleance tried to rejoice but could not. Macbeth was a great man gone bad, a brilliant general greedy for power, a soul that should have blessed Scotland but had cursed her instead.

Mary was limp and pale in a doorway. Fleance put his arm around her. "Where is Seyton?" she whispered.

"Hell," said Fleance briefly. He pulled her close to his heart so she would not see Macduff yank the sword out of Macbeth's heart, then chop off the man's head. When the deed was done, and the head had been rammed on a spike, the cheers went up, hailing Prince Malcolm king. Malcolm began a speech about the great rewards he would give everyone, and how all Malcolm's thanes from henceforth would be called earls.

My father would have been an earl, thought Fleance.

There was silence while men waited to hear their honors, and through the quiet, a muted howl filtered down from the tower of Dunsinane. It sounded like the owl that night at Inverness, when all the sounds of earth and heaven cried out against the death of Duncan. *Help, help,* quavered this owl.

"'Tis the Queen's ghost," said Fleance into the silence. "She died of her own hand. She is become a corpse screaming."

Even royal Malcolm, harsh Siward, and victorious Macduff blanched.

No soldier was going to climb to that top floor. Not where a corpse called for help.

"Come," said Fleance to Lady Mary. "The clouds have been lifted from Scotland's shoulders. The sky is blue again, and the sun shines." He took her arm and they walked together out the gates of Dunsinane.

. . . let me infold thee
And hold thee to my heart.
ACT I, SCENE 4

MALCOLM, SON OF DUNCAN, NOW HAD THE HONOR, LOVE, obedience, and troops of friends for which Macbeth and his lady had killed. The celebration feast was laid, not in cursed Dunsinane but out in the meadows, where the wind was warm again.

"And now," said the new king, "we have a different kind of score to settle. Lady Mary of Shiel, come forward."

Fear attacked Mary. The bright green gown of Lady Ross felt gaudy and large. I suffered so much at the hand of our last king, thought Mary, only to be summoned to the feet of another king? Am I now to pay for the sins of my father Cawdor?

Fleance took her arm.

"No, Fleance. I have to face it alone."

"Why? Who wants to face things alone? We will go together and hope to find Malcolm a good and gracious king like his father Duncan."

They knelt before the King of Scotland.

"I give you back Cawdor, Lady Mary," said King Malcolm, "and I assure you that Shiel has always remained yours. Fleance, the lands of Lochaber stay with you, and you, too, shall be an earl."

Mary was stunned at his generosity. Malcolm had to pay the

wages of an army of ten thousand — repay the King of England — replant the burned fields — restore the ruined homes from Macbeth's reign — and yet he returned wealth to a defenseless girl. She could not speak for gratitude.

"Fleance has asked for your hand, Lady Mary," said the new king, smiling. "Neither one of you is of age and neither has a father or guardian. That puts you both in my care. I approve the betrothal."

Mary began to laugh. Fleance kissed her while the troops roared their approval.

"I am told, Lady Mary," said the King, "that this will be your fourth betrothal. A high number for one so young. You are a dangerous woman."

"And Fleance," said Mary of Shiel, "is a dangerous man."

AUTHOR'S NOTE

THE REAL KING MACBETH RULED SCOTLAND IN THE ELEVENTH century. An historian named Holinshed wrote about him in 1587, and William Shakespeare read that book when he wrote his famous play. Shakespeare added a lot of excitement to Holinshed's story and discarded a lot of the facts. He made up his own Macbeth. Shakespeare also made up his own Middle Ages, preferring magnificent stone castles (at a time when they were wooden) and fine gowns, trumpets, and letter writing like those of his own time, roughly 1600. So Shakespeare's *Macbeth* isn't history and isn't fact. It is drama, and it is tragedy.

I read both Shakespeare and Holinshed, and then I made up *my* story, adding characters like Lady Mary, Ildred, Swin, and Father Ninian. I expanded Seyton, who is a Shakespeare character, but

Shakespeare does not identify him or anybody else as the third murderer. So my book isn't history and isn't fact, either – but it's as close as I could get to the play.

The quotes throughout *Enter Three Witches* are from the Harcourt, Brace edition of *Macbeth.** I changed contractions like *on't* or *'gin* or *o'th'* to *on it, begin,* and *of the.*

Shakespeare is the most quotable author ever to write in English. You can carry the lines of Shakespeare with you through life. It was such fun to scour *Macbeth* for lines that exactly fitted the action in *my* version. (I'm still sorry about several wonderful lines I didn't find a place for.) You will have seen that the quotes I chose may come from a different scene in the play or refer to a different character. That's the joy of quotes – they're yours. Use them often and everywhere. (Only one place looks like a quote and isn't – the rhyme on page 153, based on Act IV, scene 2.) I have also used Shakespeare's dialogue within my writing, as on page 222, for the speech of Lady Macduff, and on page 258, for Macbeth.

Now read Shakespeare's *Macbeth.*

A play is boring when it is read silently, because those lines are intended to be spoken. Read Shakespeare out loud. Act as you go. It's more fun when the whole class does it, and everyone takes a part or trades parts, but you can do it alone. Buy a Shakespeare edition with footnotes to explain words we don't use anymore or words we do use but use differently. (Don't waste your time with Shakespeare rewritten in modern slang.) When a line doesn't seem to mean anything, saying it out loud a few times usually gives you the sense of it.

The supernatural names I use are from a list written by the poet Robert Browning, who said that the women of the Scottish countryside believed in "devils, ghosts, fairies, brownies, witches, warlocks, spunkies, kelpies, elf-candles, dead-lights, wraiths, apparitions, cantraips, giants, enchanted towers, dragons, and other trumpery." I never found out what he meant by elf-candles or dead-lights, but I used them anyway.

*Copyediting was done from the Washington Square Press edition of *Macbeth*, edited by Louis B. Wright and Virginia A. LaMar, 1959.